# CURVY GIRLS CAN'T DATE SURFERS

KELSIE STELTING

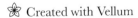

*For Annie, a beachy ray of sunshine*
*in the middle of the mountains.*

# CONTENTS

## ONE

## APRIL

I'VE NEVER HAD a dog in my life. But here I was, walking our new neighbor's golden retriever down a foggy private beach.

We'd only moved to California two days ago so my dad could get better medical care, but my mom was determined for me to "get out there" and find my community, despite the fact that military brats didn't find community—they just learned the ropes well enough to last until their next move. And my next move was only a year away.

A seagull landed a few feet away, and Heidi yanked at the leash, nearly dislocating my elbow in her chase.

"Heidi," I scolded, hanging on tighter to the leash. "Leave that poor bird alone."

She glanced back at me just long enough to show her smile and shake out her shaggy golden coat, completely unbothered by my chiding.

This dog was going to be the death of me, and it was only day one.

I slipped out of my sandals, hooking the straps in my free hand, and let my feet press against the hard, wet sand along the shore. Living on the beach was new for me. My dad had been stationed in Hawaii when I was only five, and I remembered the squishy mud more than anything else. Other than that, we'd bounced around bases in the South and the Midwest for all of my childhood.

The salty air stung my nose, still cool this early in the morning. Tiny beads of moisture hydrated my skin, and I could feel it making my wavy hair grow wild. I wondered what I looked like to all the people who lived in these beachside houses. Surely they knew how out of place I was.

Each home was bigger than the next with wide windows and massive patios facing the water. Part of me still felt uneasy here. This was our first big home since Mom's online business exploded— before this, we'd always lived on-base. Nothing like our new three-story home just blocks from the water.

A dark spot appeared in the fog ahead, and I braced myself to say hello, maybe meet one of our new neighbors.

An older guy came into view, a smile on his tanned face. "Morning," he said.

I nodded in reply.

As soon as he passed me, I let out a relieved breath. A quiet walk was exactly what I wanted.

Heidi yanked on the leash again, the loop slipping from my hand, and she took off at a sprint into the fog.

"Heidi!" I yelled, panic filling my voice. I couldn't lose the Pfanstiels' dog. Not the first day. They'd hate my family for as long as we stayed here. "Heidi, come back!"

I took off after her, barely able to see her through the fog. I had no idea what had caught her attention, but I swore I'd bury it if I ever found out.

"Heidi!" I yelled, already breathing hard.

I was *not* a runner. Not even close.

She splashed into the water, covering her coat, and went under a wave.

"Heidi!" I screamed. I could swim, but not well enough to save an eighty-pound dog. Not that I was close enough anyway. She had to be at least two hundred yards away.

Her head popped above the water, just as a surfer came in on a wave. He crashed off his board to dodge her, saltwater flying around them and showering around her golden head.

The guy came out of the water, his black curls soaked, his dark eyes on the dog. He circled his muscular arms around her, lifting her from the water. Waves crashed against his back as he walked her back to the shore, Heidi in one arm, his board in the other. The closer he got, the more of him I could see—tan abs, board shorts slung low on his hips, strong legs with a sprinkling of dark wet hair.

He got out of the water and grabbed on to her leash while undoing his surfboard from his ankle and easily tossing it farther ashore.

Realizing I was staring, I looked down at the ground and walked to them as quickly as I could, trying to catch my breath. My chest was still heaving when I reached them.

"Thank you so much," I said. "I was so worried about her."

"You shouldn't have let her run off like that," he snapped, folding his arms across his muscular chest. "I almost hit her with my board. We both could have been seriously injured."

I jerked my head back at his attack. "Like I lost her on purpose? The dog took off on me!"

A muscle in his jaw twitched. "Then maybe you should've been paying more attention."

"I should have been paying more attention? Maybe you shouldn't be surfing on a day with low visibility! There could have been kids out here!"

He quirked a cocky eyebrow. "At seven on a foggy morning?"

I narrowed my gaze. Did this guy think he owned the beach or something? Because last I was told by our overly perky realtor, it was HOA property. "Heidi has as much of a right to be here as you do."

He scoffed, turning his head to the side. "You're referring to yourself in third person?"

I grabbed the leash from his hand. "Heidi's the dog," I snapped, tugging the wet dog back toward her owners' house.

"My apologies, Heidi," he called after us. "Wouldn't want to confuse you with a reckless pet owner."

If I were five, I would have stuck my tongue out at him. But I'd just turned eighteen, and I was livid. So I lifted my middle finger in the air and kept walking away, wet, traitorous dog in tow.

# TWO
## DIEGO

MY PULSE WAS STILL RACING as I went back and sat on my surfboard. I'd barely seen that dog, Heidi, in time to bail, and I'd been terrified my board would hit her anyway.

Luckily, Heidi was okay. Me on the other hand?

I lay back on the board, taking slow, steadying breaths. Maybe it was just because I was angry, but the sight of that girl walking away? It had my head torn in all kinds of directions. The swing of her hips had been so *distracting*, and—

"Diego!" my mom called. "Breakfast is almost ready! Go shower off and get dressed!"

I blew a raspberry through my lips and got up, carrying my board back to the house. I leaned it against the garage wall and used the outside shower to rinse off. Then I went into the bathroom and took off my shorts, hanging them on the drying rack. I slipped into a fresh pair of shorts and a T-shirt, running my hand through my hair so my curls wouldn't clump, and started up the deck stairs.

Through the glass patio doors, I could see all my family already at the table, along with my older sister's new boyfriend, Jude Santiago. It was weird, having a famous singer in our house, but my sister was kind of famous now too.

Jude lifted his hand in a wave. "Sit by me, man."

I slid onto the bench next to him and said, "Only if you promise to keep your hands off my sister in front of me."

Jude laughed. "We'll see if she can keep her hands off me."

Des hit his side.

"See?" Jude said.

Dad rolled his eyes at the both of them, hiding his amusement.

I shook my head, reaching for one of the breakfast burritos Mom had on a platter in the middle of the table. Then I waited for my younger sister Marisol to finish with the salsa verde, so I could put some on my plate.

Mealtimes had always been chaos with three

younger siblings and one older sister, but my parents said they were the most important time of the day. So we always sat together, whether it was breakfast before school or a bedtime snack at the end of the day.

I ate while Mateo, Marisol, and Adelita attempted to teach Jude how to say all the items on the table in Spanish. When he said *cucaracha* instead of *cuchara* for spoon, they all burst out laughing.

"What?" Jude asked. "What did I say?"

Eight-year-old Mateo crooned, "You said you're eating your food with a cockroach!"

Mom gave them an admonishing smile while Dad shook his head.

"Learning a new language takes practice," Dad said. "Mateo, it took you eighteen months to learn to say 'Mom' instead of 'Dom'."

We laughed at the memory, and Mateo's cheeks reddened. "I was just a baby."

Des reached across the table, tickling his shoulder. "Still are the baby of the family."

He stuck his tongue out at her.

Mom cleared her throat. "I got a letter from Emerson Academy today, Diego," she said.

I raised my eyebrows. "Did they say I get to skip college counseling? Because that would be great."

Mom shook her head. "They said this year they're giving seniors the option to volunteer at the school on Fridays or take a class from Emerson Technical College. You could be a CNA or study cosmetology or even train to get a CDL since you're eighteen. You could work as a truck driver while you figure out your next steps."

I raised my eyebrows at her. "I barely got my license last year and you want me to drive a semi?"

Dad said, "I don't see you with any other plans after graduation other than hanging out on that surfboard. Teaching lessons on the weekends isn't exactly a viable full-time job, Diego."

My muscles tensed up. Here was *the talk* again.

The lecture where I got reminded that graduation was coming and I needed to figure out a career if I didn't want to go to college.

But my problem? I didn't really have dreams, and I wasn't good enough at school to like the thought of spending years at college to figure it out. Surfing was fun, but I didn't want to compete. I loved teaching lessons, but it didn't make enough money to move out or pay for much of anything in the "real world" my parents were preparing me for.

This constant pressure was making me miserable. "If I take one of those classes, can we stop talking about my plans for next year?" I asked.

The entire table seemed to go quiet, waiting for my parents' response. Mom and Dad exchanged a glance, having one of those silent conversations between themselves. Finally, Dad looked at me and nodded. "Just pick one."

"I'll be a CNA," I said, digging back into my burrito.

Des seemed surprised. "You picked just like that?"

"Yeah," Mom agreed. "Don't you want to see the program details?"

I shook my head. "I'm not driving a semi, and going to the salon with Mom gives me a headache."

"Great," Mom said with a smile. "I'll fill out that paperwork tonight."

I nodded, finishing up my breakfast. "Is it okay if I go back out? I have a lesson coming at ten."

They nodded, and I went outside, ready to be back in my happy place again.

# THREE
## APRIL

THE NEXT MORNING didn't start off too badly—
Heidi had stayed on her leash for our walk and I
hadn't run into Mr. Thinks-He-Owns-the-Beach.
But the day was still young, and my nerves were
going wild for my first day at Emerson Academy.

I walked in the back door and hung my jacket
on the hooks before walking into the kitchen,
freezing in the doorway. Dad sat at the table, eating
a slice of toast and drinking coffee across from
Mom, who had her laptop out and was doing work.

She looked up at me, her smile bigger than I'd
seen it in a long time. "How was your walk?"

"Good," I said, cautiously stepping into the
kitchen. Dad hadn't been awake this early in

months. Much less in a good enough mood to sit with us and eat breakfast.

He smiled up at me. "Morning, monkey."

The nickname nearly brought tears to my eyes. Since my name was April, they'd shortened it to Ape, and that led to the monkey nickname. He hadn't called me that in so long. "Morning, Dad. How are you doing?" I asked tentatively, hoping I didn't say the wrong thing.

"Good," he replied. The shadows coming through the kitchen windows made the scars on the left side of his face seem deeper. But there was a familiar look in his eyes too, like he was my dad again. "Ready for your first day with all those rich kids?" he teased.

I snorted, feeling lighter than air. My dad was joking with me again? Maybe this doctor was already helping him! "I think so. Other than the uniform. What kinds of kids wear blazers to school?"

He stiffened, and I froze. What had I said wrong?

*Uniform*. Such a big part of his career.

A trigger.

Mom said, "Ape, why don't you go upstairs and get dressed."

I stalled, not sure I wanted to leave Mom alone with this.

"Go ahead," she said, a false sense of cheer in her voice as she shut her computer and put it in a drawer.

I backed away from the kitchen, knowing arguing would make it worse, and started up the stairs.

Just as I reached the third stair, I heard Dad's rising voice, Mom's hushed murmurs as she tried to soothe him. At the seventh stair, I heard the crack of plastic on tile. We knew better than to buy breakable dishes now.

I covered my mouth to hold back my cry. This wasn't fair. None of it was. Not to Dad or Mom or me.

When I crested the stairs, another crash sounded, and I flinched. Quickly, I changed into my new school uniform: a navy pleated skirt, light blue button down, and a navy blazer to match. I squeezed into my navy stockings and black leather shoes, then grabbed my makeup bag and backpack.

I waited at the top of the stairs, trying to get a sense of what was going on downstairs. A door slammed, shaking the house, and then it was quiet. My ears perked for any further sound, any argument. Hopefully this was the end—the part where Dad went to his room and watched TV to cool down. He and mom hadn't shared a room since his injury.

Mom came to the bottom of the stairs, holding a towel to her hand.

My heart squeezed. "Did he hurt you?" Usually Dad didn't direct his anger at us, but if he'd injured Mom...

She shook her head. "I pinched my hand on the drawer when I was putting my computer away. I'm fine, honey." She waved her joined hands, signaling me to come downstairs. I tiptoed as quietly as I could, the leather soles of my shoes seeming to scream against the modern metal stairs.

As I got closer, I could see the moisture in my mom's eyes. The wrinkles and dark circles no amount of makeup could hide. These last few years had aged her beyond comprehension.

"Are you okay?" I asked.

She sniffed, avoiding my gaze by reaching into her pocket with her uninjured hand. Pulling out a twenty, she said, "I'll pack you a lunch tomorrow. Promise."

I nodded, holding back tears of my own. "Maybe go work at a coffee shop today?"

She glanced over her shoulder toward the bedroom. It was hard for her to leave him alone, but that's why we had home cameras installed. "I'll try."

She wouldn't.

But it was a lie I needed to hear to get me out the door. "I'll see you after school."

"Actually, the Pfanstiels are hoping you'll walk Heidi twice a day. Apparently, she does a lot better with more exercise."

Before I could protest, she walked me to the front door, handing me my keys from the rack. "Have a great day, Ape. This school is going to be something special for you. I can feel it."

No matter how much I disagreed, I gave her a quick hug and walked to my car.

Since I didn't know the town well enough yet, I turned on directions on my phone and followed them, only stopping at a gas station to apply a coat of makeup since I'd been in too much of a rush to do it at home. I was already big—putting on a face of makeup helped me blend in.

I drove until I reached an ornate building. It was intimidating—all brick walls and stone pillars and fancy cars in the parking lot.

My last school in Kansas wasn't anywhere near

this fancy. It had been a basic high school with more kids than chairs in the building. Only a few came from rich families—in fact, most of my peers had picked on the students driving these kinds of vehicles to class.

But now I was one of the "rich kids." This car wasn't brand new, but it was from this decade with not a scratch in the paint or an imperfection in the upholstery. Mom said I deserved to have something nice, but I think she was just happy to give me something after war had taken so much away from us.

I found my assigned spot—unlucky number thirteen—and turned the car off. Any military brat knows you don't step foot on new ground without observing first. So I looked out the windshield and waited. There was a crowd of underclassmen hanging out around a bench, greeting each other after a summer away from school.

Farther in the parking lot, a group of kids about my age hung out around a pickup. Some girls sat on the tailgate while guys clung around them. The popular crowd—they were at every school.

Most people, though, just crossed the parking lot to the courtyard and went up the cement stairs into the building. Overall, it seemed safe enough.

So, I got out of the car, keeping my gaze forward. Making eye contact was just an invitation I didn't want to give, whether for friends or enemies. My breath came hard by the time I hit the top of the stairs, and I breathed deeply to catch it. Weight was an easy target for most bullies, and I didn't want to give them any fuel.

"Are you new here?" someone asked.

It sounded like a teacher's voice, so I turned to the left, seeing a woman in a white dress covered in a red apple print. She had an apple on her headband and dangly pencil earrings. Suddenly, I wasn't the biggest target in the vicinity, and I breathed a sigh of relief.

"Yes. I'm—"

"April Adams, right?" she asked. At my nod, she smiled. "I met your mom on Monday. She's a peach."

Maybe this woman just really liked fruit?

"I'm Birdie Bardot, the guidance counselor here," she continued. "You can call me Birdie."

I raised my eyebrows, not used to teachers being so familiar with students. Most of them acted like using their first name was a crime against the natural order of the world. "Nice to meet you," I said, just in case she hadn't forgone all social customs.

"Same to you. Come with me; I'll show you around."

I readjusted my backpack on my shoulder. "Thanks."

"This is your schedule." She passed me a piece of paper and walked to the heavy oak doors all the students were entering through, a sea of navy and light blue much like the ocean looked this morning.

I glanced down at the paper as I followed her over the tile floor. English, math, current events, and physics. All pretty standard. Then my electives were after lunch—art, videography, and personal finance.

"Your mom said you should like these classes," Birdie said over her shoulder, "but if you get a few days into it and decide you want something different, let me know."

I studied the page a little closer. "What's this about Fridays?"

She stopped outside a wooden door with the name Birdie Bardot, Guidance Counselor, on a golden nameplate. "Those are our flex days." She pushed the door open, leading me into a room with a desk, filing cabinets, and a big white bird in a cage. The bird looked at me curiously.

"That's Ralphie," she explained.

I nodded. Animals weren't really my thing— especially since Heidi had nearly broken my elbow and completely embarrassed me yesterday.

Birdie reached for a pamphlet on her desk and passed it to me. "This year, we're trying something new. Seniors can choose to volunteer on Friday afternoons, or they can choose a vocational skill to learn." She tapped on the middle page where there was a bulleted list.

I read down the items—and my eyes widened. "I could really get a CNA?" I'd wanted to get the certification over the summer, but plans fell through with the move.

Birdie nodded. "Is that what you'd like to do?"

I grinned, feeling my chest relax a bit. "That would be great."

The warning bell rang, and it sounded old, like an actual bell made the sound, not like the stereo beep from my last school.

"I'll sign you up for CNA classes then." Using a feather pen, she wrote something on a bright pink sticky note and then said, "Come with me."

We walked around the building, stopping by the

doors to each of my classes as the hallways thinned. When the second bell rang, she led me down the main hallway, stopping by an open classroom door. "Mrs. Morgan," Birdie said, stepping inside. "This is your new student, April Adams."

"Welcome!" Mrs. Morgan said. She had on a flowy black skirt, a black top, and seemed way more even-keeled than Birdie. "Introduce yourself to the class."

Birdie waved goodbye, telling me to come to her office if I needed anything. Hating this part, I turned to face my peers, about to begin my prepared speech...until right in the middle row, I saw my worst nightmare.

That guy from the beach was in my class and staring right at me.

# FOUR
## DIEGO

I LEANED BACK in my chair, taking in the girl from the beach.

*April Adams.*

Instead of the shorts and T-shirt she'd been wearing the day before, she had on our school uniform. That plaid skirt was doing things to her hips that weren't fair to guys like me.

Her eyes widened and then narrowed on me, all that spice from the day before back in full force. I couldn't help but smirk at the memory of her middle finger in the air, and I found myself thinking something that never helped a situation with an angry female.

*She looked cute when she was mad.*

April quickly looked away from me and introduced herself like she'd practiced the speech a million times before. "I'm April Adams, just moved here from Kansas."

A guy sitting in the back row mooed, and the rest of the class laughed. At the way her face fell, I clenched my fists under the desk. What was wrong with people? I glanced toward the back, seeing a guy from the football team named Tate grinning as one of his friends high-fived him.

"California has cows too, you know," Mrs. Morgan said, more exasperated than angry. *Why wasn't she angry?* "Thank you, April. Why don't you take that seat?"

She pointed to an empty desk at the front of the room, and April sat, slinging her backpack over the back of her chair. Her brown hair fell to her shoulders in waves, flatter than it had been that day at the beach. And instead of flipping me off, she had her hands in her lap, resting on her thighs.

Mrs. Morgan had Faye, the girl sitting next to April, pass out the syllabus for the semester. I took the sheet, setting it on the desk in front of me, and tried not to stare at April while Mrs. Morgan went over the rules for the year.

April's family had come here from Kansas?

Why? What else had she planned to say about herself before Tate made fun of her?

And, more selfishly, was she really that mad at me?

Would she come to class every day hating my guts? I had been kind of a jerk back on the beach, even if I had been scared crapless. I resolved to apologize to her after class. Hopefully we could start over.

As soon as the bell rang, I grabbed my backpack and followed her to the crowded hallway. She had squeezed herself against the opposite wall to avoid people passing by, but I followed her and tapped her shoulder so she'd wait up.

When she looked over her shoulder and saw it was me, her eyes narrowed. "Yes?"

"Hey." I gave her a nervous smile. I always smiled when I was nervous—it seemed to make people ease up. But not her. Her eyebrows just drew closer together.

I cleared my throat. "I wanted to talk to you about yesterday," I said at the same time a pair of arms flung around my shoulders.

A flurry of blond hair flew in my face. "Hey, you!" Kenzie said.

"Hey," I replied with a grin, hugging her back.

Kenzie looked between April and me. "Sorry, I was just so excited to see you! I haven't seen you all summer!"

April shook her head and turned to walk away.

"Wait up," I said, about to tell Kenzie I'd catch up with her at lunch.

"Looks like you're occupied," April replied and continued down the hall.

Kenz looked after her, frowning. "Who's that?"

"New girl," I said simply, not wanting to think about my failed attempt at an apology. "Tell me about Greece. Did you fall in love like that girl from the Traveling Pants?" (My sisters had made me watch that movie at least a hundred times.)

She shoved my shoulder. "You first. You spent your summer hanging out with a rock star! I need the tea on Jude and Des. Are they really in love or was it all publicity?"

"Oh, it's real, all right." I shuddered at the visual of them making out on the beach. "But he's a good guy. He's good to her."

"That's amazing!" Kenz said. "Please tell me you'll let me meet him soon. I need to get every-thing autographed—my poster, my phone, my face."

I rolled my eyes at her, and she laughed.

The bell rang, interrupting us, and she said, "I'll catch you at lunch. I have an idea for a halftime stunt that could be really fun, but I need some of your muscle."

I flexed under my jacket. "I have some of those."

She laughed and flounced away, and I went to health class with Mrs. Hutton, dreading yet another round of syllabus day.

Outside of the classroom, I saw Tate leaned up against the locker, talking with one of his idiot friends like he hadn't just ruined April's first day. "Hey," I snapped.

"Hey, man," he said, lifting his hand for a high five.

I stared at it, watching him slowly bring it down to his side.

"What's up?" he asked, unsure of himself for once.

"Mess with the new girl again, and I'll make sure you feel it at football practice."

He lifted his hands in defense. "Sorry, I didn't know you had something going on with her."

"She doesn't have to be my girl for you to treat her like she matters."

# FIVE
## APRIL

MY THROAT FELT tight as I walked to my next class. I didn't know what beach guy had wanted, but it couldn't be good.

The day had already gotten off to an awkward start. I didn't know whether that guy was mooing about my weight or the last state I lived in, but I knew it only took one person to open the floodgates, and I really didn't want to spend my senior year getting bullied about my size.

Not when I was already worried about my mom, still grieving my dad who I'd lost in all the ways that counted, stressed about applying to colleges, and navigating a new town.

But I knew I was "safer" in a classroom than I was in the free-for-all hallways, so I counted down the door numbers until I reached statistics. The teacher up front introduced himself as Mr. Aris and had me introduce myself to the class. Some of the students were the same from English, but some were new, so I repeated my spiel, adding that I was an only child and was born in Germany.

"We're glad to have you," Mr. Aris said, smiling warmly.

The next couple classes went the same with introductions and syllabi. Starting at a new school at the beginning of the year was easier in some ways than jumping in halfway through. Everyone was getting used to a new routine, not just me. But as far as I could tell, I was the only new student here.

Emerson Academy seemed like the kind of place that was part of your identity. Not just a school someone attended because they were in-district. Being here meant something. I just wasn't sure what it meant to me. Not yet.

On my way to the lunchroom, I wished I could disappear. Seniors and juniors had the second lunch period, and I'd made a meaningful connection with... nobody. Not that I was the best at making friends.

My mom had been the biggest constant in my

life, my rock when my dad was deployed and my anchor when he came home injured. Most people just didn't understand. And the ones who did had their own lives to worry about.

I gave the cashier my money, and she gave me a receipt with change. I picked up one of the navy-blue trays, lightened with scratches and use, and took it through the line, filling my plate with things that caught my interest.

I did have this to say about the Academy: their food looked a heck of a lot better than some of the things I'd been served in public schools.

I took my tray and scanned the small cafeteria full of round tables for an open spot. I wished the tables were longer—that way you could sit a few seats away from people and get your space. It was like they wanted you to actually talk to other people with this setup.

Someone nudged my arm, and I quickly apologized, stepping away. Just as I realized it was the same guy from the beach, the same guy from English, I backed into another person. But this time, their tray flipped.

Hot soup, crackers, and a sandwich with mustard went all down my side, burning my skin and completely ruining my clothes.

The girl I'd bumped into apologized, but I was already on the verge of tears.

"Come on," the guy said. He took my hand, his encompassing my own, not giving me a chance to argue. I followed him out of the lunchroom and down the hall, not completely sure where I was.

"That was so humiliating," I whispered, mostly to myself. Now everyone would either know me as the moo-girl or the one who'd been soaked with food her first day. I just hoped the person I ran into wouldn't be out for revenge.

"Are you okay?" he asked.

I took my hand away from his, pausing in the empty hallway. "No, I'm not okay!" I said, tears streaming down my cheeks. "I'm pretty sure I have third-degree burns from the soup, I'm starving because I didn't have time for breakfast, didn't get to eat my lunch, and now I've embarrassed myself in front of you, twice! I wish you would just stop showing up!"

His brown eyes seemed to soften, and I looked away, feeling guilty for my outburst. This mess wasn't his fault.

"Come on," he said gently. "I'm sure Birdie has some extra clothes."

Feeling guilty for blowing up at him, I followed

him down the hallway. He didn't have to help me after all. But here he was. *Why?*

I didn't have much time to come up with a reason before we reached that same wooden door from earlier. Birdie was standing in front of Ralphie's cage, saying something I couldn't quite hear. When the guy knocked on the door, she looked up, smiling at him. But when her eyes traveled my way, her smile fell.

"Oh, honey," she said, frowning. "Let me get you a fresh set of clothes." She patted the guy's arm. "Thanks for bringing her here, Diego. I've got it."

*Diego.* I rolled the name over in my mind, wondering if it matched his personality.

He seemed to stall, like he didn't want to leave.

"Everything okay?" Birdie asked.

He glanced between her and me, biting his lip. "You know what you did for my sister?" he asked.

Understanding sparked in Birdie's eyes. She nodded.

"I think you need to do it again."

I didn't know why they were talking about his sister when I was covered in soup and mustard, but luckily, Birdie said, "I will," and Diego left her office.

She reached into her cabinet and got out a fresh uniform. "Come with me."

Thinking I had reached rock bottom, I followed her across the hall and into the gymnasium. The orangey-yellow hardwood floor had Drafters written down the sides in navy-blue paint with an emblem of a feather quill.

We reached a door on the north side of the gym, and she said, "This is the girls' locker room. You can change in there. Towels are by the shower stalls."

She passed me the uniform packaged in a clear bag with a 3XL sticker on top.

"How did you know my size?" I asked.

She shrugged. "Your mom picked up your uniforms two days ago—still fresh on my mind, I guess."

Not wanting to spend any more time covered in food than I had to, I walked into the locker room, praying no one was in there. But when I rounded a wall of lockers, I froze. A girl with turquoise hair sat on a cement bench, eating a packed lunch with her phone playing a TV show.

She jumped at the sight of me, then seemed to relax when she realized I wasn't a teacher... or a jock. "You scared me," she accused.

"Didn't mean to," I mumbled, getting a towel and then locking myself in the bigger bathroom stall. First, I slipped out of my shoes, peeled off my wet knee socks. I sucked in a breath, dropping the wet mess to the floor. There were already red spots on my leg from where the soup had hit. Then I unbuttoned my skirt and let it fall to the floor, kicking it aside. I twisted, eyeing the mess. Hopefully it wouldn't stain.

I ripped open the plastic bag, put on my new outfit, and then went to the sink. As I checked myself in the mirror, I could see the girl's eyes on me.

"Someone dump food on you?" she asked.

I reached for a paper towel, watching it turn dark brown under the stream of water. "Bumped into someone."

The wet brown paper felt heavenly against my leg. I ran it up and down the burn, from my mid-thigh to a third of the way down my calf.

"No one to bump into down here," she said and took another bite of her sandwich.

"Except you," I replied, a slight smile on my lips.

She lifted her eyebrows in concession. "True."

We were both quiet for a moment, and I tossed

the paper towel, going back to the bathroom stall to finish changing. With the door shut and locked, she said, "I'm Sadie."

I focused on the buttons of my shirt. "April."

"I know. I saw you in current events."

I hadn't seen her; my head had been down through most of my classes anyway. I finished changing and laced my shoes back up. Carefully balling my clothes so the wet, dirty parts were on the inside, I walked out of the stall. I wasn't sure what I should say to Sadie, but she was looking at her phone again.

I walked back out of the locker room, where Birdie was waiting, and prayed for the day to hurry up and end.

# SIX
## DIEGO

I PULLED MY HELMET OFF, letting the wind hit my sweaty scalp, and went to the water table for a drink. The first day back at football practice had been rough. Usually I spent the summers surfing and that kept me in shape, but I'd been on tour with my sister and Jude for three months this summer. I'd worked out, but it wasn't the same.

I poured myself some water and then dumped a second cup over my head. Some girls giggled in the stands. I grinned up and winked at them. If they were watching, might as well give them a show.

This was my last year in high school, my last year without responsibilities, as my parents liked to remind me. Why not enjoy it?

I turned away from the stands, seeing the cheerleaders practicing off the field. Kenzie waved at me, and I lifted my hand in return.

"Diego," Coach yelled. "Get your eyes off the skirts and get back on the field."

I cleared my throat and braced myself to go run more lines.

After another half hour of running, Coach called us to center field and gave us a pep talk, but I only heard half of it. I just wanted to go home and cool off in the water.

When everyone started walking back toward the school, I followed along, walking between my friends Xander and Terrell.

Terrell bumped his helmet against mine and said, "My parents are going to Boston this weekend to see my sister, which means..."

I grinned. "Party?" He didn't let loose often because his parents were on the stricter side, so we always made good use of their time out of town.

He nodded. "Seaton Beach? Around nine?"

I lifted my chin. "I'll get the word out."

Xander said, "I'll talk to my brother about a keg." He and his older brother often got into trouble together because their parents were always busy with their family business. Something in software that made ridiculous money, but not enough to buy time with their children.

"Perfect," Terrell said just as we reached the locker room. I took a quick shower, changed into some shorts and a T-shirt, then went back outside. Kenzie was waiting by my car with her friend Deena.

"Hey, you," Kenzie said.

"Hey."

She frowned. "You look rough."

"Gee thanks," I said, cracking a smile.

"Do you mind if Dee and I catch a ride with you? My car's at the shop."

"Get in," I said. Her house was just a few blocks from mine, so it wasn't a huge inconvenience or anything.

Deena crawled into the back seat, answering her phone as she did. "Hey, baby!"

I gave Kenzie a questioning look. "Who is it this time?"

"New college boyfriend," she explained.

I nodded and focused on the road, pulling out of the school parking lot. Kenzie and Deena were best friends, but I never really got to know Deena well because it seemed like she was always on the phone with a boyfriend. Always an older guy. Always a piece of crap.

"So Greece," Kenzie said. "I've never gotten a worse sunburn in my life."

I laughed. "Most people come back with a magnet or something."

"I have that too. But no romance was happening for me there. My parents had me babysitting my little sister practically the whole time. Once the guys saw me with a twelve-year-old, they steered clear of us."

"Probably a good idea," I said over Dee chattering in the back seat. It sounded like she was the one carrying the conversation.

"But the food was *amazing*, and the vibe was so laid back everywhere. The water at the beach was like bathwater and so clear—not cold and fishy like it is here. I'm trying to convince my parents to send me to college there."

I nodded as we drove along the road, trying to pay attention. Trying not to wonder if April would be walking by my house again. Wondering why I cared either way.

Dee laughed loudly in the back seat, distracting me from my thoughts. Kenzie and I both looked back at her and she blushed, covering her face. *Sorry*, she mouthed.

I looked forward again, taking the turn to Kenzie's street. She lived a few blocks back from the beach.

"Diego," Kenzie said like she was repeating herself.

"Sorry, yeah?"

"I was asking if you wanted to practice that stunt this weekend?"

"Sure." I rubbed the back of my neck, trying to get myself back to normal. "Party at Seaton Beach on Friday, by the way. Can you invite the squad?"

She stuck out her tongue. "You just want some cute girls there, don't you?"

"Always," I replied. I stopped in her driveway behind her mom's Miata. "See you later."

"Later." She got out of the car and bent over. "Thanks for the lift."

Dee waved at me through the open door, still on her phone.

"Any time," I replied.

I drove back to my house and found I was the only one there. Dad usually worked until dinner time, and according to the wall calendar, Adelita had dance practice tonight, which meant Mateo and Marisol were probably with our grandparents.

Des and Jude were back to work in LA, recording their new duet. I missed having her around, even though I liked that she was living her dreams.

If only I could find mine.

I took my board to the water. My legs felt like rubber from practice, but as soon as I was on the water, I felt light again.

The cold liquid stung my skin and brought me back to life as I lay against the board and paddled out. About fifty feet from shore, I stopped and just sat on my board. This far out, the houses started to look small. The noises of town disappeared. All I could hear was lapping water, singing birds, and my own breath.

For the first time all day, I felt at ease. Like I was exactly where I belonged.

If only the feeling could last.

## SEVEN
## APRIL

I KNOCKED ON THE PFANSTIELS' bright yellow door to return Heidi from our evening walk. As I waited, I braced myself to tell them that I couldn't walk Heidi anymore. She had been wild, chasing every seagull she could spot, and I was completely exhausted. Between school and home, I just didn't have the energy to do this too.

Mr. Pfanstiel, a tall, thin man with wispy white hair welcomed me inside. "How did she do?"

"You know Heidi," I said, a guilty feeling sweeping over me.

Mr. Pfanstiel chuckled. "I certainly do." He bent slowly like it hurt him to get that low and undid Heidi's leash. She sprinted toward the water dish and food bowl, lapping up both in record speed. "I really appreciate this. With my hip and Phyllis's job, it's harder to get her the exercise she deserves."

My heart melted slightly. "Your hip?"

He nodded. "I'm only sixty-two, but my doctor's saying I'll need a hip replacement within the year. If we didn't have you, we might have to rehome her, and that would just…" He shook his head, sadness in his eyes.

The fact that he cared so much about his pet made me like him more. And feel that much guiltier for wanting to give up on Heidi. I couldn't give up on her. Not when it would hurt the Pfanstiels so much to find another option. Placing a smile on my face, I said, "I'm happy to help. I think my mom just wants me out of the house."

He cringed as he sat on a chair at their kitchen island and then chuckled. "When my kids were teenagers, they were always out of the house. It was all my wife and I could do to get them to sit down for a dinner together."

"How old are your kids?" I asked, leaning on the counter across from him.

"Forty-two, thirty-eight, and twenty-nine. Now

we get all the time with the grandkids we could ever want."

I smiled at his natural use of "we" even though I hadn't seen or met his wife yet.

"Your mom said you're a senior, right?" he asked.

I nodded. "I just turned eighteen."

"I have a sixteen-year-old granddaughter who lives in LA. Maybe you two can meet sometime."

"Sure," I replied, knowing it would probably never happen. Or matter if it did. I'd be gone in a year. I just hoped someone would take my place to walk Heidi.

"I better get back home," I said.

He nodded. "Take some cookies with you?" He patted his flat stomach. "My wife made some, and if they stay on the counter, I'll be eating them all before the grands get here."

"I'm not about to turn down cookies," I replied with a smile.

He waved his hand and went to the corner of the kitchen. Just as he'd mentioned, there was a plateful of cookies resting on the countertop. He reached into a cabinet and pulled out a plastic bag, his hands shaking on the seal. It took all I had not to offer my help, but he eventually got it open and packed it to the brim with the cookies.

Then he reached into his pocket, opened his wallet, and pulled out a twenty-dollar bill.

"You don't have to do that," I said. I definitely didn't need the money. Mom's business was making more than enough to support us. "It's nice to just walk on the beach."

He pressed it into my hand, then held out the bag of cookies. "Every kid deserves some money they don't have to ask for. Enjoy."

I smiled. "Thanks, Mr. Pfanstiel."

"Jesse," he said with a smile. "Same time tomorrow?"

I took a deep breath and smiled at the man. "Absolutely."

When I got outside his house, the sky was tinged pink with the sunset. Jesse lived on Coral Loop, and I walked east until I hit Starfish Lane. My footfalls blended with the constant crash of the ocean. It had been so quiet in Kansas, but here there was always background noise.

I walked a little farther from the beach and saw the peach-colored home that was officially ours. Its dark blue shutters and white trim seemed so stark in the dimming light.

The front curtains were open, and I looked through the picture window, seeing Mom on the couch, her legs tucked under her and her laptop on her thighs. As I got closer, I could see the bandage on her hand, the lamplight glowing on her face making the circles under her eyes seem darker.

As if she could sense me, she looked up and smiled. She got up from the couch and met me at the door, taking me into a big hug. "How was your day? Did you make any friends?"

I held up the cookies in my hand. "Just Jesse."

She cupped my face with her hands, drawing them over my hair, and pressed her forehead to mine. "I'll get some milk."

I went upstairs to my room, changing into pajamas, then went back downstairs. Mom was sitting outside at the patio table, and I joined her, enjoying the fresh air. So far, the weather here had been a big improvement from the last few places. Kansas had been so windy, Colorado had huge weather changes from scorching heat to freezing cold, and I'd felt like a fry in the oven in Oklahoma.

Mom nodded toward a cup of milk on the table. "That's yours."

"Thanks," I said. I reached for an oatmeal chocolate chip cookie on the plate and dipped it into the milk. "How was Dad after I left? Did you make it to his appointment?"

She chewed on her cookie for a moment. "Dr. Sanders thinks he should be in a day program."

The cookie instantly felt like soggy cardboard in my mouth. "What does that mean?"

Without any inflection in her voice, Mom said, "I'd drop him off at eight in the morning and pick him up at five, starting on Monday."

"Like a daycare?"

She gave me a look.

"I'm not against it," I clarified. "I think it would be good for you and him to get a break from the house. But do they know how he is any time you ask him to do anything? Especially if you interrupt his sleep..."

"The idea came from Dr. Sanders, and Dad agreed in the office."

"He won't remember," I said dejectedly, looking down at my cup. Crumbs floated in the milk.

"She did say there are options if he decides he doesn't want us taking him. They could have someone come pick him up."

I raised my eyebrows. "A stranger in the house, bossing him around?"

Mom's shoulders sagged. "I know."

Seeing her so defeated made my chest hurt. "We'll figure it out, Mom."

Her smile was sad as she looked up at me. "We always do."

## EIGHT

## DIEGO

XANDER WALKED beside me out of the school. The second we hit the parking lot, he dropped his skateboard on the asphalt and rode slowly beside me. "I can't believe you chose CNA classes," he said.

"It sounded better than the alternative," I replied.

He raised his eyebrows, making them disappear behind his shaggy brown hair. He didn't believe me. In fact, he thought he had it made by getting assigned to volunteer with the elementary gym class on Fridays. "You just added more homework to your plate, dude."

"It got my parents off my back," I said finally. Mostly because I wasn't looking forward to it either.

I loved *mis abuelos*, but I'd never spent much time in hospitals or retirement homes. This wasn't exactly the path to my dream job.

We reached my car and I stood by the door. "Have fun in gym class. I'll see you at practice."

Xander nodded and kicked his skateboard up to hold it. "See ya. Wouldn't want to be ya." If he wasn't already walking to his truck, he would have seen me roll my eyes.

I got in my car and typed the address for Emerson Technical College into my phone. It was just a ten-minute drive, right by Marisol's violin lessons, but I'd never been to the campus before.

Even though I didn't admit it to Xander, I was happy to get away from the Academy for a couple hours. At school, expectations were everywhere. Birdie had already scheduled an advising appointment with me, just a month away. The first football game was coming up in a week. And now Kenzie wanted me to practice that stunt on the weekend. Not to mention the constant reminders from our teachers that college was quickly approaching.

As I drove away from the Academy, I could feel myself relaxing. And with a certification under my belt, maybe my parents would back off of the future talk, at least for a little while. I'd have a job to do at least while I figured things out.

"Destination is on your right," my phone said. I almost missed the gray sign for Emerson Technical College and realized why I'd never noticed it before. The colors didn't really stand out at all. But now, I took in a big auto-shop like garage, a parking lot full of cars, and a decent-sized building.

I looked at the email with directions on my phone and followed them to the main doors that led into a drab building. There were halls full of classrooms, and I stopped outside the one with a big yellow sign.

WELCOME CNA STUDENTS

Readjusting my backpack over my shoulders, I walked inside the room with four rows of long tables. There were a handful of people there, mostly women, but my eyes landed on one. April.

Her lips were parted, staring at me. But as soon as the shock wore off, her gaze narrowed. She didn't want me here.

I'd been so distracted, I hadn't even noticed the teacher sitting at her desk in the front corner of the room.

She studied me over the top of her dark-rimmed glasses. "Hi, can I help you find your class?"

"This is it," I said. "CNA right?"

She nodded. "Take a seat. We just have a couple more people coming."

I walked toward the back of the room, and April picked her backpack up from the floor, putting it in the open chair beside her.

*What the heck*, I wanted to ask. Just because I called her out for almost injuring the dog and me, I was now public enemy number one? I had helped her in the lunchroom, after all. And I'd yelled at Tate for picking on her—he hadn't so much as looked at her in English class since Monday. Whatever. If she wanted to play it that way, she was more than welcome to. I didn't have to care.

I didn't have to be bothered.

Not by some new girl who barely knew me at all.

I shook it off and sat at the table behind her. She kept her eyes straight ahead. Fine. *Fine*.

A couple more people filtered into the room, and the teacher stood in front of the whiteboard. "This is our group," she said. April and I were the only ones there from the Academy.

She uncapped a marker, the plastic squeaking, and pressed the tip to the board.

Janice Miller, RN-BSN.

"My name is Janice Miller. You can call me Mrs. Miller or Janice. I worked in doctors' offices as an LPN, licensed practical nurse, for twenty years. Once my kids graduated high school, I went back to school too and got my LPN to RN and then my RN to BSN—Bachelor of Science in Nursing. There are going to be a lot of abbreviations coming at you, so I encourage you to always have plenty of notetaking paper and a pen."

I reached into my backpack and got some out.

"We come from all different walks in this class, much like the people you'll be serving as a CNA. Some of you are high school students just looking to fill an afternoon. For some, this will be your first real job in medicine, a building block to a fulfilling career. For others, a career as a CNA is the goal, and trust me, it can be very rewarding."

Ahead of me, April nodded. I wondered which one she was—if this was a way to pass the time or a means to an end.

"Over the next twelve weeks, we'll learn some of the basics of caring for others as a CNA, you'll take a certification exam, and then you'll get hands-on experience at a clinical site to become certified in the state of California. Any questions?"

Someone up front raised her hand and said, "I don't have a sitter next Friday. Can I bring the materials home?"

"We allow two absences as long as you complete the makeup work. Any more than that, and you'll have to take the class over again."

A few other people asked questions about the schedule or clinicals, and I just sat back watching, observing. Then Janice said, "Let's go around the room and introduce ourselves. Tell us your name and why you're interested in becoming a CNA."

I sat back in my chair, listening as the people up front told their stories. She was right; all of them were different. The mom from earlier was expecting a second child and wanted a way to earn extra money. Some were college students wanting patient care experience for med school applications. One guy said he needed a job and this one paid decently. And then it was April's turn.

She turned sideways in her seat, facing the group as she said, "My name's April Adams. Someone in my family suffered a TBI a few years back, and the nurses were like a rock for my family. I want to give that to someone else, and this is a great way to gain experience before nursing school."

The room grew quiet as I digested that information. I wasn't sure what a TBI was... I was so busy thinking it over, I almost didn't realize everyone was waiting on me to go. I cleared my throat and said, "Hey, I'm Diego. I signed up because I didn't want to get a CDL."

Everyone laughed. Everyone except for April.

Janice seemed amused. "Fair enough. Hopefully you made the right choice." She winked. "Next?"

Once everyone was done with introductions, Janice passed out our textbooks, and we got started on the first section: professional communication.

I'd never been in a three-hour long lecture before, but the time seemed to drag on and on. I was glad when she told us to close our books and pack up.

Now I just had football practice, and then it was time to let off some steam at the party on Seaton Beach.

# NINE

## APRIL

AFTER THINGS WENT SO BADLY at lunch on Monday, it seemed safer to share the locker room with Sadie. Now I knew that had been a mistake. We hadn't talked much throughout the week—she watched her show, I worked on homework—but on Friday, she took out her earbuds and said, "There's a party tonight."

She said it like pointing out the sky was blue or that skunks smelled bad. So I wasn't really sure how to reply. But then she added, "It might not be completely lame to go."

I still wasn't quite sure what to say, so I just nodded.

"I can pick you up," she said again in that matter-of-fact way.

So that's why I was now standing in front of my bedroom mirror, debating what to wear.

Completely hopeless, I texted my mom to see if she wanted to come upstairs. I would have yelled down to the living room, but loud noises set off my dad, so it was always better just to text since we always kept our phones on vibrate.

Within a minute, Mom came upstairs. She frowned when she saw me.

"I knew it was bad." I sat on the bed. "I should just text Sadie and tell her I'm sick."

"Boo you, wh—"

"*Mom*," I said, laughing despite the *Mean Girls* reference. We must have watched that movie together at least twenty times.

"You look adorable," Mom said, folding her arms across her chest and looking at me like she might one of her digital designs. "It's just a little..."

"Dark?" I asked. I had gone with a black shirt and dark jeans.

"Plain," she replied. She went to my dresser, which I'd unpacked my very first day here, and rifled through the draws. She pulled out a pair of lacy cream-colored shorts and threw them my way. The tag fluttered as they sailed through the air and landed on my lap.

"These are way too short," I said. "I told you that when you bought them."

"There's nothing wrong with showing a little leg!" She winked.

*There was when your thighs were as thick as mine*, I thought. But Mom would have scolded me to no end if she heard me say that out loud. She was all into body positivity and pushed me to have a good self-image. And I did. For the most part. But I was a teenager; I had eyes. You didn't get to be eighteen in 3XL clothing without knowing how most people treated big girls.

She left my dresser and went to my closet. After flipping through a few shirts, she brought out a denim shirt with long sleeves. "You can roll the sleeves on this, maybe pair it all with your tan sandals? You'd look so adorable."

"I'll try it," I said. I ripped the tag off the shorts and then changed into them while Mom looked through my jewelry tree.

"Tell me about Sadie. You haven't said much about her."

What was there to say about Sadie? "She's quiet." We'd exchanged maybe ten words with each other, and most of them happened earlier today.

Mom listened for more.

I pulled off my top and reached for the button up. "She likes sitcoms. Like old ones." In fact, she'd been watching *Golden Girls* every day this week.

"Sounds like my kind of gal," Mom said. She held up a bronze necklace with a dark brown pendant. "Try this too."

I took it, draping it over my head, and Mom rolled my sleeves for me. With both of them up, she stepped back, taking me in and smiling. "The boys are going to be all over you."

I snorted. For all the romance movies we'd watched together, I'd never had a boyfriend. I'd never even kissed a guy. And considering the only guy I "knew" at Emerson Academy had a blond, model-type girl all over him, the odds were looking slimmer than ever.

As Mom fluffed out my waves, she said, "You never know what could happen, Apie. One day you're walking through life, and then all of a sudden someone changes everything."

I looked up at her, seeing the tired lines around her dark blue eyes. "Is that what happened with Dad?"

She pulled her lips to the side, nodding. "For all

the hard times we've had, it's important to look back and remember we had good ones too."

And then I asked the question I never should. Because I had to know. "Was it worth it?"

She smiled, her lips faltering, and then a car horn sounded outside.

I slapped my hands over my mouth. I'd forgotten to tell Sadie not to honk or ring the bell.

"Have a good time, honey," Mom said, rushing me out of my bedroom. If Dad was awake, we didn't have long. "I'll see you by two?"

I nodded. "Promise."

She followed me down the stairs, whispering, "Remember, if there's alcohol there and you decide to drink—"

"No driving. Call if I need you." We'd been over it a thousand times. "I love you."

I gave her a hug at the bottom of the stairs and turned into the living room just in time to see Dad staring out the front window, his jaw tight.

"Who is that?" he snapped and scratched along the scruff of his chin, agitated. "It's almost nine o'clock. I need to go outside and tell them to keep it down. People are trying to sleep. God damn inconsiderate son of a—"

"Doug," Mom said soothingly. "I'm sure it was a mistake."

He stepped back from the window, and his eyes narrowed on me. "Why is Ape dressed like a stripper?"

Mom turned to me. "*Go.*"

I felt guilty as I ran to the door.

"I'm her parent too!" Dad roared. "You send her out dressed like that? What a worthless mother you are!"

My hand froze on the handle. I knew irritability was a symptom of his TBI and PTSD, but to hear him tear down the woman who had done *everything* for us...

"Stop it!" I yelled at him. "Just stop it!"

He raised his hand, coming at me, and Mom stood between us.

"Go, April!" she shouted.

Dad took her arms, trying to get around her. But Mom was a big woman who could hold her own.

"GO!"

I walked out the door, tears stinging my eyes.

Sadie was waiting in her car, and I ran to the passenger door, knowing I didn't have time to stand around and get these stupid angry, guilty, devastated tears to go away. I got inside, and when I wiped at my face, Sadie said, "Everything okay?"

It was the first real question she'd directed my way. But all I said was, "Just text me next time."

## TEN

# DIEGO

"HERE YOU ARE," Kenzie said, handing Xander and me red Solo cups. "Made it special for you, Di."

That was our code that meant she poured the soda without any alcohol. Most guys at Emerson went crazy on the weekends, mostly because they could steal from their parents' liquor cabinets without them noticing. But I didn't like the way alcohol made me feel out of control.

I thanked her and took a drink of the soda, sweet and tangy bubbles pouring over my tongue. She sat down in the sand next to me, leaning back against a big piece of driftwood next to the fire.

Terrell sat across from us, holding out his cup. "Cheers."

Xander, Kenzie, and I tapped our cups to his. "One heck of a party," I said. Between the smell of the beach, the warmth still in the sand, and the light coming from the fire, I didn't think it could get any better.

Terrell scanned the beach. There had to be almost fifty people here from our school, and the night was still young. "Gosh, I love this. The only thing I don't understand," he said, "is why someone always plays a freaking guitar at a party."

"Gotta show off to the chicks," Xander said with a smirk that said he'd be playing guitar if he could. But he already got plenty of attention from girls at the skate park or on the football field.

Kenzie shook her head at them. "I think it's nice. Adds to the ambiance."

"Of what?" I asked. "A fire and the waves are good enough."

"For the guy who could live on his surfboard, I'm sure it is," she retorted. "The rest of us enjoy the real world."

"Ha ha," I said.

Deena came over with a cup and her phone in hand, sitting next to Kenzie.

"No boyfriend tonight?" I asked.

Kenzie gave me a warning look, but it was too late. Deena burst into tears.

Terrell, Xander, and I exchanged confused glances. "What did I do?" I asked.

"H-h-he dumped me," Deena sobbed. My heart sank for her. Kenzie confided to me once that Deena had disordered eating, and getting compliments from guys helped her feel good enough in her skin. I hated that she couldn't find that confidence in herself.

Kenzie patted her back. "He's a jerk. You're better off without him."

Terrell pushed up from the sand. "I think that's my cue to bounce."

I shook my head at him. He only had one sister, and as far as I knew, she didn't deal with a lot of heartbreak. He wasn't great with emotions. But living with three sisters, emotions were all I knew. So I leaned over Kenz and put my hand on Deena's shoulder.

"Hey," I said, my voice firm enough to get her attention.

She seemed stunned as she sniffled and stared at me.

"If I learned anything from my older sister, it's that some guys can be real jerks. But if you waste your time worrying about them, you'll miss out on the guy who really cares."

Her eyes softened. "You're so right," she whispered.

"Of course he is," Kenzie said. She nudged my knee with her elbow, hissing, "Keep going."

Okay, time to improvise.

"You know there are one-star reviews on *Titanic*, right?"

Deena sniffed. "Because it has a terrible ending."

"It's based on a true—you know what? Never mind. My point is it's one of the most popular movies in all of history, and there are still people who say it's terrible. Just because someone doesn't see your value doesn't mean it isn't there."

Deena reached over Kenzie and wrapped her arms around my neck. "Thank you, Diego. You're just the best, trying to cheer me up like that."

I patted her back. "Anytime. You need to enjoy yourself tonight. Have a good time. You can do that without some loser guy."

"I promise." She pulled away, taking another drink from her cup.

Xander nudged my side, whispering, "What kind of kung fu magic was that?"

I shrugged, about to reply when Kenzie spoke.

"Is that the new girl with Sadie?" Kenzie asked, tilting her head toward the hill everyone had to walk over to get here.

Sure enough, Sadie and April were walking toward the party, but my eyes glazed right over Sadie's aqua hair and landed on April. She had on these short shorts that showed off her hips and thighs. They swayed back and forth as she walked down the hill, and I had to look away before my body started taking over where my mind left off.

"Do you have any classes with her?" Kenzie asked.

Deena hiccupped. "We have current events together. She's pretty quiet."

Kenzie nodded. "I had to partner with her in art, and she barely said two words to me."

The guy playing guitar changed songs to an acoustic version of "Macarena".

"Oh. My gosh!" Dee said. "We have to dance to this!"

She pulled Kenzie's hand, and Kenzie yanked my hand. When I protested, she growled, "If I have to do this, so do you."

Begrudgingly, I got up and went with them to

dance. Xander laughed at me, getting up to go hang out with other non-dancing people. Lucky.

To be fair, I liked dancing. You don't grow up in a Mexican family and not know how to dance. But it wasn't exactly the impression I wanted to leave with April. Although, I didn't know why I cared so much. She clearly didn't care about me.

But here I was, girls on either side of me, swinging my hand through the air like I was throwing a lasso.

When the music changed to a slow song, Deena put her arms around my shoulders. "Wanna dance?"

Her words were already slurring.

"Are you sure you don't wanna go home with Kenz? Have some ice cream? Chocolate frosting? Watch *Dirty Dancing* a few times?"

Deena giggled. "You are so sweet, Diego. I don't know why I didn't notice that before but—"

"Um, I have to go pee," I rushed out, stepping away from her. I practically ran to the darker part of the beach, hoping she wouldn't follow me. I didn't want to give Deena the wrong idea.

My heart didn't slow until the sand became wet under my feet. I let out a long breath.

"Are you following me?"

I turned, seeing April's outline farther away from the waves. "I didn't even know you were here."

She was quiet for a moment. "So you signing up for CNA classes had nothing to do with me."

My eyes were adjusting to the darkness, and now I didn't understand how I could have missed her creamy legs standing out in the moonlight. I drew my eyes up and focused on her face. "Get over yourself, Adams," I said. Angry at her for being so rude. Angry at my mind for being so damn distracted by her body.

"You're the one who thinks you own the beach, and you want me to get over myself?" she snapped.

I barked out a laugh. "You're still going on about this? It was one day." She needed to let it go.

"One day can change everything," she replied, her tone serious.

"Clearly, because the day I found out you were going to Emerson, my year changed for the worse."

Her mouth fell open into an angry half-smile, and she looked away. "You are, without a doubt, the most arrogant person I've ever met."

"As arrogant as the one saying I'm stalking her?"

She narrowed her eyes at me, coming so close I

could smell her perfume. Sweet, like honey, but sharp like ginger. "You can just leave me alone."

"You want that?" I asked, looking down at her, seeing all of her curves.

Her throat moved with her swallow. "*Please.*"

"At least now I know you have some manners." I backed up a few steps and returned to the party.

## ELEVEN

## APRIL

I STARED open-mouthed at Diego's back as he walked away from me. He had on a thin white T-shirt that showed far more of his muscled physique than his school uniform did. Sand lifted from his feet in small bursts with each step.

Feeling embarrassed for staring, guilty for being rude to him, I turned back toward the water and plopped in the sand. The ocean was a big rolling black mass except for the white caps where the waves broke.

"Hey," Sadie said.

I glanced over to see her walking toward me, two red cups in her hands. She handed me one and sat beside me. For a moment we were quiet until

Sadie took a drink from her cup and said, "Beer is awful."

I took a drink of mine and cringed. "You're right. It's terrible." I laughed as I tried to mouth away the taste. "Why do people act like this is so cool?"

She nestled her cup in the sand and leaned back, her long turquoise hair tickling the ground behind her. "I don't know why I thought a party would be a good idea. I hate most of the people at school."

"You don't go to parties?" I drew my legs to my chest.

"Why do you think I eat in the locker room?"

"Because you can watch TV that way," I replied.

Her laugh was harsh. "That's just a perk of not being judged for eating."

The words cut at every insecurity I always tried to fight. Usually, I was one of the biggest girls at school—it was strange to have someone I could actually commiserate with. "Who cares what they think?"

She gave me a look. Conversation over.

"We should go," I said, standing up. I didn't want to be here either, acting like everything was fine. Even though my mom had texted me that she was okay and Dad calmed down, I still felt on edge.

"Where would we go?" she asked.

I shrugged. "What do you usually do on a Friday night?"

"Probably hang out at my mom's pottery studio."

"Let's do that then." I extended my hand to her.

She let me help her up. "My parents will be there."

It was like a punch to the gut, knowing she could spend time with her parents. That her mom wasn't constantly pushing her out the door and her dad wasn't a stick of dynamite with an instant fuse. I caught myself in my pity spiral. Comparing my life to hers would only make me resent her, and she'd been nothing but kind to me. "Are they nice?" I asked.

Sadie nodded. "They'll be thrilled if you came over. That's kind of why I came to the party tonight —they think I need more socialization. They'd want me to join a club or something if I didn't get out more." She shuddered as if organized socialization was even worse than the hormone-filled mess going on up by the bonfire.

I laughed. "Clubs aren't so bad." I'd been in a

few before, but I tried not to join them anymore because I didn't want to let anyone down when I had to move again.

"Try sitting through an hour of chess club, watching pawns move back and forth, and you'll change your tune."

I laughed, digging my toes through the sand as we stood by the rolling ocean. I didn't want to walk by the party... didn't want to face *him* again. Every time I opened my mouth, it just got worse. "Can I ask you something?"

"Sure."

"What's the deal with Diego?"

Her silence was suspicious. Made me feel suspect.

"I don't have a crush on him or anything," I said quickly. Which probably didn't help matters.

"Sure," she said again. Even with how dark it was, I could see the twinkle in her eyes.

"It's okay; forget I asked." I began walking back toward the party.

She let out a breath, making me stop. "Diego De Leon... A Leo. Six feet, two inches tall. Tight end on the football team but doesn't play any other sports. Average in school... Kind."

"Kind?" I raised my eyebrows disbelievingly.

She nodded. "Out of all the guys in our class, he's the most decent. I think it's because his older sister was a bigger girl. And very outspoken. She probably would have been all over him if he'd done something rude to a girl like her. Or anyone for that matter."

So he was just rude to me...

"And I'm sure you want to know if he's single," she said.

"Nope." Because I already knew. He was either taken or a complete player. I'd hardly seen him without a girl hanging on his arm. That blond one seemed to be around him the most though. Because of course that's the kind of girl he'd be into—model thin, big blue eyes, pouty pink lips, and long blond hair. She was beautiful—objectively, not in the obscure kind of way that required perspective.

She couldn't have been more opposite from me.

"So the studio?" Sadie asked.

"Right." I followed her through the sand, back toward the source of the music and party noise. We passed right by the spot where Diego was sitting by the fire, surrounded by three girls and a couple guys. They were laughing, having fun. And he refused to meet my eyes. I felt pathetic for digging for info from Sadie. I clearly wasn't as interesting to him as he was to me.

April and I got back into her car, and she drove about fifteen minutes away to a well-lit street of shop buildings. Most of the storefronts were closed, but the upper levels were full of light.

Noticing me looking, Sadie said, "Most of the second stories are apartments, but Mom rents one for her art."

"Is she an artist?" I asked. "Like full time?"

She nodded. "Mom and Dad mostly sell her pottery online and at craft shows, but they've done bigger projects too, like installations in new buildings."

"That's cool. My mom's an artist too. Well, kind of. She makes digital prints to sell online. People buy them on T-shirts, coffee mugs, that sort of thing."

"Nice. The art gene completely skipped a generation with me."

"Same here. But I haven't really tried pottery yet. Aside from that one bowl I made in second grade. Shoddy craftsmanship. Zero out of ten."

Sadie's laugh made me smile. It was the kind of laugh that started in her belly and scratched up the back of her throat. Completely unique, just like the rest of her.

We walked up a stairwell on the back of the building, and when we reached the door, I could hear music coming from inside. Something that sounded old and happy. Sadie pushed the door open, revealing one spindly woman with pink hair deliberately painting a dark red piece of clay, and a rotund man, spinning clay at a table, brown hair falling over his face and his hands covered in muddy water.

"Sadester," her dad said, looking up. "You're back early."

Her mom cleared her throat. "Arlo, she brought a friend."

The wheel slowed and he swiveled his head. If he'd been a DJ, the music would have screeched to a halt. Instead, "Love Shack" by The B-52's scored the moment.

"This is April. She's new at school, and party was lame, so I thought I'd show her the studio." Sadie turned and gave me half a smile. "Maybe help her make a replacement for that clay bowl from second grade."

This place, these people, seemed to make Sadie

come alive. I wondered if I'd only seen a part of her at school, but this was the real Sadie.

"Welcome," her dad said, wiping his hands on an apron at his waist. "I'm Arlo. This is my partner, Harini."

The woman smiled, coming to shake my hand. "So nice to meet you, April. You know the origin of your name means 'opening buds of flowers'?"

"I-uh—"

"Mom's into the meaning of names," Sadie explained. "She looked it up as soon as I told her about you." She blushed as if she'd said too much.

"I'm also interested in belly dancing, personal finance, the lifecycles of hummingbirds, dog behavior, yoga... one can never have too many interests," Harini said. "Now, do you really want to make a bowl or is there something else that interests you?"

I glanced around the studio, seeing racks of pottery, from simple coffee cups to intricate vases and jewelry. A memory of the clattering plate echoed through my mind. "Maybe I can make a coffee cup as a gift..."

Arlo stood up from his chair. "Great place to start. Let me get a new brick of clay."

"And an apron," Harini said.

Soon, I was outfitted with a paint-stained apron

and sitting on a chair in front of the pottery wheel. As the clay shaped beneath my fingers, I couldn't help but think of Harini's introduction.

"So you said you're interested in dogs..."

She gave me an instruction on moving the clay and said, "Absolutely. Our Bichon's over there sleeping."

I followed the tilt of her head and saw a small, fluffy white dog resting on a colorful dog bed.

"Why do you ask?" she said.

"Well... I know this dog..."

TWELVE

DIEGO

I FELT like garbage when I woke up. Not from drinking but from lack of sleep. After dropping off Deena, Kenzie convinced me to practice cheer stunts with her on the beach. She said it was better to practice on the sand since it would give her a soft landing. And she pointed out we only had a week left until the first game.

My siblings were playing upstairs—I could hear the thunder of their feet above and their peals of laughter. Even though Adelita and Marisol were twelve and thirteen, they played with our eight-year-old brother Mateo like they were his age instead.

"Diego!" Mom called down the stairs.

I groaned, throwing my arm over my face. I

knew I couldn't sleep with all the racket upstairs, but that wasn't going to stop me from trying.

"DIEGO!" she yelled even louder.

"I'm up!" I called back, rolling begrudgingly out of bed.

I threw on a pair of shorts and a shirt, then used the bathroom before going upstairs. My hair was a complete mess, but I didn't have anywhere to be. Yet.

As I trudged up into our main living area, Mom called from behind the stove. "You know the rules. You can stay out late—"

"But you have to be ready to get up early," I finished with a yawn. "I know."

Adelita and Marisol sprinted past, and I raised my arms overhead. "I'm not a traffic cone."

Mateo ran straight into my midsection, falling over backward. Shaking my head, I reached out my hand, and he used it to scramble up and chase after them. A second after he ran away, my eyebrows drew together. "Was he wearing..."

"Your sister's dance costume? Yes." Mom rolled her eyes. "I swear, sometimes... Here, the eggs are almost ready. Can you start rolling the burritos?"

I nodded and went to the sink, washing my

hands again, even though I'd just done it in the bathroom. If Mom didn't see it, it didn't happen.

"How many are you making?" I asked, staring at the giant pan of eggs.

"Your sister has to be on the bus with her team in an hour and a half," she said. "I agreed to make breakfast for the girls."

I raised my eyebrows. "An hour and a half? Mateo was just in her costume."

"I know. We have a lot to do, so be fast."

While Mom and I rolled burritos and wrapped them in foil, Dad got the girls and Mateo ready to leave. Mom stopped working in the kitchen long enough to do Adelita's hair, and then they left for the bus, a red cooler full of food in tow.

The rest of us didn't have to leave quite so early to watch her dance, so I showered and changed into nicer clothes. After a while, we entered a completely different world.

Sometimes I joked that Adelita's dance competitions were like a cult. All these little girls flounced around in matching sweat suits, all the moms looked stressed out, and the dads seemed bored out of their skulls. Plus, everything smelled faintly of hair spray, kind of like the church smelled of incense on Christmas and Easter.

But I liked seeing Adelita dance. Even from my seat, I could tell how much she loved it—she put all of herself into the movements, and even during the serious or emotional parts of the routine, there was a small smile on her face.

Dad, Marisol, Mateo and I entered the ballroom filled with chairs and edged our way into the fourth row. Soon *Abuelo* and *Abuelita* joined us, then *Tio* and *Tia* De Leon. They didn't have any kids of their own, but they always supported their nieces and nephews. They'd be at my game next week, cheering me on with a GO DIEGO sign, no matter how much I told them they didn't have to.

Dad held up his program and said in Spanish, "We still have half an hour until Adelita's turn."

*Abuelita* reached into her purse, pulling out a coin purse and carefully sorting out quarters. "Diego, will you go get us a snack from the vending machine?"

I nodded, used to being volunteered for different tasks. "What would you like."

She smiled, her dark eyes nearly disappearing. "Surprise me."

I promised I would and got up, dropping the quarters in my pocket. Upbeat music rang in my ear as I walked back down the aisle into the massive hotel lobby. It took a bit of searching, but eventually I found a vending machine.

I scanned the items, trying to find something with peanuts in it—*Abuelita* loved nutty desserts. I was about to press the button, when I heard a feminine voice say, "Hey there."

I turned, finding a girl about my age in a black track suit. Her hair was pulled away from her face, her lips were painted bright red, and her eyes had thick blue eyeliner.

"Sorry," I said. "I'm just about done."

She leaned against the side of the vending machine. "Take your time. I'm enjoying the view." Her grin informed me that, yes, she was flirting.

I tossed her an easy smile of my own before putting in the quarters and choosing a candy bar.

"Where are you from?" she asked.

"Emerson."

"Brentwood. I knew you looked familiar. I'm on the cheer squad, and it's hard not to notice you on the football field."

Chuckling, I bent down to grab the candy bar. "I'm sure they'd forgive you for wanting to cheer on the winning team."

Her cheeks grew pinker underneath the blush she was already wearing. A lot of girls reacted like that to me—blushing, smiling. It made April's reaction all the more confusing. Why was she so determined to dislike me?

I was so busy thinking about the way April treated me at the party that I completely missed what this girl was saying. "Sorry, what?"

"I was saying if you wanted to hang out sometime, we should. I'm free most Sundays."

I bit my lip, thinking about her offer. She was cute enough, but I didn't want a girlfriend who would demand all of my time. I saw the way my guy friends disappeared once they got a girlfriend, and I didn't want that to happen to me.

"I'm pretty busy," I said, hoping to spare her feelings. "But I can't wait to hear you cheer me on at the game." I winked and walked away, going back to my family.

My time this year was meant for one thing: enjoying what little freedom I had left.

MOM and I stayed up late Sunday night, packing a bag with all the things Dad would need for his first day at the day program and more. I could feel the nervous energy in our home, even if we didn't speak much about it out loud.

Dad being out of the house for eight hours a day would be huge for Mom and her business. No more late nights spent with a fresh pot of coffee in front of a glowing screen. No more constantly backing up her computer in case one of Dad's episodes took a different turn. No more worrying about how they were while I was at school.

But there was more to consider... How would Dad do around new people? Our family, his schedule, and the occasional doctor visits were all he'd known for the last few years. How would he do around strangers? Waking up early? Coming back home at the end of a long day?

I hoped this would be good for him, bring more joy to his life too, but our lives never seemed to be that simple or straightforward anymore.

Mom and I set Dad's things for the next day by the front door, and I slept restlessly all night, worries on my mind until my alarm clock went off in the morning. Relieved to be in motion, I rolled out of bed and got ready.

With my clothes on and backpack ready, I went downstairs to meet Mom in the kitchen. She had a chocolate croissant for me that I could barely eat with the nerves dancing in my stomach. It tasted like cardboard, and I had to drink lots of creamy coffee to get down the flaky dough.

Both of our plates were empty, but Mom and I just looked at each other.

Her breath was shallow. "Are you ready?"

I shook my head.

"Me neither." She stood up anyway and put our coffee cups and plates in the sink. I pushed in our chairs, and we walked to Dad's bedroom, the one right off the living room. I stared at the white door, lines up and down its length.

Mom reached for the handle and gently pushed it open because knocking would disturb him. The room was completely dark with blackout curtains. "Doug?" she said softly.

He rolled under the blankets. Dad had been a big man before his accident—six feet, four inches tall, and two hundred and twenty pounds. He stayed fit for his job in the military. But now his muscles had softened, his belly had rounded. He was big and every bit as intimidating as a bear when he wanted to be.

"Doug?" Mom repeated.

He mumbled something.

"Remember Dr. Sanders said she wanted you to try the day program today?"

Dad said, "Today?" His voice was still hazy with sleep.

"Yes, she wants you there at oh-eight-hundred." We still used military times with each other, because it was all we knew.

"What time is it?" he asked, his voice clearing slightly.

"Seven. Enough time to grab a shower and a breakfast before we go."

"We?" he asked.

"Yes, I'm driving you, remember?"

"Right," he replied. "Wish I still had my license." Around the corner of the door, I saw him pushing up, sitting on the edge of the bed.

"I know you do," Mom said gently.

He rubbed his face, then shuffled to the bathroom and closed the door.

Mom let out a relieved breath.

And I was relieved too, but my heart ached. Dad had lost so much.

Mom whispered to me, "Will you set his pills out while I get his clothes ready?"

I nodded, going to the kitchen and grabbing the container with his pill bottles. He took something to prevent seizures, another for nerve pain, one to prevent blood clots, another to make sure fluid didn't build up in his brain, and another one for his mood. The pills didn't fix everything, but when he didn't take them, things got so much worse.

I selected the right amount from each bottle and put them in a little plastic condiment container that I carried to his bedroom with a cup of water. Mom set the pills on his nightstand by his clothes at the head of the bed, and we stepped out of the bedroom. She closed the door just in time for the shower water to stop.

We glanced at each other, and Mom held up

crossed fingers. She stepped away from the bedroom door, going to stand by the front door. "Can you bring my backpack and your dad's bag to the car?" she asked.

I nodded, taking the bags from her. "Anything else?"

She shook her head and held the door open for me. I took my time walking to the car in the driveway and popping the trunk. The only thing in there was a folded-up cane. Dad didn't need it very often, but it was nice to have—it was easier to deal with crowds when he had the cane to remind people to steer clear, but now we hardly went out at all.

I walked back to the door, but Dad and Mom were already coming outside. Dad was dressed in a pair of newer jeans and a dark blue T-shirt. His hair was still damp, combed over slightly.

"Hey, Dad," I said with a smile. "Looking good."

"Thanks, kid." His eyebrows scrunched together. "Aren't you supposed to be in school?"

"I was so excited to see the day program, my teachers said I could come in late." I fidgeted with the hem of my skirt. "I hope that's okay."

"Well, I..." He cleared his throat, glancing to

Mom, who was now beside him. "I guess that would be alright."

"Great," I said. "I'm going to drive behind you guys so I can leave from there. See you soon." I forced a smile, acting like everything was okay when in fact, my heart was breaking.

This would be good for him—his doctor told Mom as much—but I couldn't help feeling like his enrollment in a day program was a failure on our part. A failure to keep him home and do what was best for him. A failure to help him heal.

I waited until I was in my car and following them to let the first tear fall, and then I wiped it away. Today wasn't about me. It was about Dad.

We drove across town to a place with a sign out front that said The Rhodora Center. A pretty pond with a grassy park on one side separated it from RWE Memorial Hospital. I noticed two people fishing off a small bridge. Others walking the trails —some in scrubs and others in regular clothes.

It didn't look like an institution, and that fact had me breathing a sigh of relief as I got out of my car.

Mom and Dad parked up front in a handicap spot, but they waited for me to cross the lot and reach them.

Dad's eyes tracked from the Rhodora Center parking lot to the hospital. "Dr. Sanders might think this is a good idea, but I'm not so sure."

Mom rubbed his arm, then held his hand. "You're going to do great, honey."

He cleared his throat but didn't shy away from her. Still, she dropped his hand, giving him some space, and we started walking.

Mom pressed the buzzer at the door and said, "Douglas Adams is here for his first day." Someone dressed in scrubs came to the heavy glass double doors and let us in.

"Doug, it's great to see you. And these are your lovely wife and daughter?"

Dad's smile was crooked, but visible, and that gave me hope. "Grace and April."

"Great to meet you. I'm Belinda, the charge nurse here. I'll give you a tour and then show you where you'll be starting today."

We walked with Belinda, trailing slightly after as she showed us around the center—there was a music area, an art room, a massive kitchen, and more. Dad was stiff the entire time, but when we got to the community area, Belinda said, "What do you think of the Rhodora, Doug?"

Dad cleared his throat. "It seems okay."

My heart twisted, searching his tone, his body language for any hint that this wasn't okay.

"Great," Belinda said with a smile. "You two have a great day. We'll get him back to you safe and sound."

Dad nodded. "Have a good day at school... and work." Then he turned around. There was no hug for Mom or me. No wave goodbye.

My eyes felt hot as Mom and I walked out of the building. We stood on the wide sidewalk that led to the parking lot and looked at each other.

"That was a lot," Mom whispered.

I nodded, wiping at my eyes. It was hard to leave him, no matter how good this place would be for him. "What now?" I asked Mom. My throat felt tight.

She pulled me into a hug, rubbing my back for a moment before she whispered, "We live our lives."

AFTER OUR ENCOUNTER at the party, I fully expected April to level me with an incinerating glare first thing Monday morning. Instead, when I got to class, her seat was empty. Even after the bell rang, she still wasn't there.

Mrs. Morgan began going over the lecture like nothing was out of the norm. So I leaned over to the guy next to me. "Where's the new girl?"

He shrugged. No help.

Why did I care anyway? School would be better without constantly encountering someone who hated my guts.

I got out my notebook and tried to take notes on the intricacies of Elizabeth Bronte's writing style. I doodled in an attempt to keep my hands busy and my mind clear, but soon my doodles turned into plays for the game Friday night.

Coach had taught us a few new plays, a couple where I ran for a pass as opposed to blocking on the line. This overwhelming sense of loss overcame me as I realized this Friday would be my last first football game... ever.

The bell rang, and Mrs. Morgan assigned us fifty more pages to read with accompanying annotations. Just one of many assignments I'd be cramming in tonight.

I got up, slinging my backpack over my shoulder. Halfway down the hallway to my next class, I felt my phone vibrate in my pocket. After checking to make sure there weren't any teachers looking, I read the text.

Xander: Dare you to grind the ramp outside before our next class.

A grin split my face, and I texted him back before even thinking.

Diego: Deal.

Just like last time, I went into the boys' bathroom, locking myself into a stall. I could see Xander's leather shoes with the brand on the side that he made from bending and burning a paperclip. Anything to be different. On the other side,

Terrell's massive feet were visible under the stall. His parents had to special order leather shoes so he'd adhere to the dress code.

We waited silently while the last of the guys left the bathroom and the bell rang. Then I heard Xander unlock his stall door.

"Just don't bust your face this time," he said.

I left my stall, facing him. "Fall one time and all of a sudden your friend doesn't trust you anymore."

Terrell chuckled. "You're lucky the seniors graduated so they'd stop calling you scar face."

I shook my head. "Let's do this before we get caught."

We walked to the bathroom door, and Xander cracked it open, checking the hallway for teachers or the hall monitor. Phil Grant wasn't nearly as bad as Pixie Adler, but he had a habit of popping up at the worst moments. Even though he had special permission to get to class a few minutes late, he should be gone by now.

"All clear," Xander said, pulling the metal door open.

We spilled into the hallway, Xander holding his skateboard close to his chest, and hurried toward the front door, ducking at every classroom so we wouldn't be seen.

At the front door, Terrell used his height to slide a sticky note between the door alarm to trick it into thinking no one had opened the door, and then we were out on the front steps, basking in the autumn sunshine.

Xander pressed the board to my chest. "It's go time."

With a smirk, Terrell said, "Want me to pre-dial 911?"

I rolled my eyes, shoving off my backpack and taking the board. I spent enough time surfing to know I could handle this, and I skated around with Xander plenty over the years. This was no big deal.

Even though the stairs were looking taller than they usually did.

I put the board on the ground while taking off my blazer—Mom would kill me if I got a rip in this one—and then got used to the feel of the board under my feet.

I could see Terrell swaying side to side. "Dude, you need to hurry up before someone catches us."

I smirked at him. "Scared?"

He rolled his eyes. Xander laughed.

I took a deep breath, gauging the distance between the school's front door and the middle railing. Then I bounced on my heels to prep myself, and kicked off on the board toward the railing.

Getting close, I lifted one leg, then pushed down and back to gain momentum.

Just like I was about to surf a massive wave, adrenaline coursed through my body, slowing everything down as I rose through the air. And then I found purchase on the metal railing, wind rushing past my body as I slid down with the grind of board against steel.

Movement flashed in my periphery, navy blue and brown. Curvy.

The distraction cost me my balance, and I swung my arms, attempting to correct myself just a little too late. I bailed from the board, missing the bottom two steps and rolling on the concrete with a big grunt as a scream pierced my ears.

Groaning, I rolled to my back, doing a mental assessment. Nothing felt broken, but my shoulder hurt like a son of a gun.

Footsteps reached me, and that citrus ginger scent hit my nose as April knelt over me, her hair falling around her face and the sun hitting her crown like a halo.

"Oh my god, Diego, are you okay?"

"Better now," I replied with a smirk.

Her worried look immediately turned to one of annoyance.

"Come on, can't smile if you're mad," I said, grinning despite the splitting pain in my shoulder.

Her lips fought all her willpower, pulling into a smile. "I hate you."

"Back at you, Adams," I replied. She was already walking away, and I didn't mind the view one bit.

Terrell and Xander ran up to me, Terrell pulling me up while Xander got his skateboard. Terrell glanced from me to the new girl and back again, a grin growing on his face.

I gave him a look. "Don't say a word."

"I wasn't going to say anything," he replied, shooting Xander a grin.

"Right, he was going to leave it to me to pick on you."

I glared at him.

Xander tapped his chin. "What was worse? That epic dismount or the botched job with the new girl?"

I shoved him just as we heard the fire alarm go off inside.

*Busted.*

## FIFTEEN
## APRIL

I LOADED my draw string bag full of dog treats I'd bought from the store using the money Jesse had given me. I was going to figure out how to walk Heidi without having my elbow dislocated if it was the last thing I did. Bonus points if she never dragged me in the direction of Diego De Leon ever again.

When I'd seen him fall from doing that stupid skateboarding trick, my heart had leapt to my throat. I was so worried and genuinely afraid that I'd have to call 911 or even perform CPR. We hadn't gotten that far in our CNA classes, and I was woefully unprepared.

Almost as unprepared as I had been from his smile.

When he lay like that on the sidewalk, with his curls all messy and the sun shining into his eyes... I almost forgot to breathe.

It was like all pretenses had been wiped away and it was just... us.

But then he had to make that comment, and the anger that had left my body came back tenfold. Why did he have to get under my skin?

I let out a deep breath as I approached the Pfanstiels' house and knocked on the door.

As soon as Jesse opened it up, Heidi came sprinting out, her leash in her mouth.

"Heidi," we both scolded at the same time.

She stood by the gate of their front picket fence, looking innocently up at us with the leash in her jaw.

"I've got it," I said with a laugh. "Is it okay if I give her treats today?"

"Completely fine," Jesse replied. "You're a lifesaver."

As the door, shut, I walked toward the gate where Heidi waited.

"You're an ornery thing," I said to her, making her head tilt and her eyebrows rise.

"Don't act all innocent," I laughed, taking the leash and clipping it to her collar. She turned her nose to the gate, excitedly waiting for me to open it so she could yank me after her.

"Here's the deal," I said. "I got some tips from Sadie's mom and a bag full of treats. Today is going to be a good day."

If she understood, she didn't let on. So I breathed deeply and opened the gate. Just like usual, she took off, eagerly pulling me from the sidewalk toward the sand. But this time, I said, "HEIDI! TREAT!"

That got her attention. She turned toward me, maybe stunned or curious, and I pulled a treat from my bag. "That's a good girl." I gave her the treat and scratched her neck. We walked just a little ways before I turned and, tugging her leash, said, "Heidi, let's go!" She followed me, and I praised her again, sinking my fingers in her soft golden fur and then giving her another treat.

For the next half hour, Heidi and I did the drills Harini told me about over and over and over again. We didn't get more than a few minutes' walk from the Pfanstiels', but sweat dripped down my brow and pride swelled in my chest.

Heidi was actually paying attention to me. Actually listening.

I dropped to my knees in front of her on the

sand and scratched her back, her shoulders, her ears, and she dragged her long sloppy tongue over my cheek.

I giggled, tugging up the collar of my shirt to wipe off the drool.

"You know, Heidi, you might be the best part of my day," I admitted, sitting back in the sand. She nuzzled up next to me, nudging her head under my arm.

I smiled slightly, petting her fur. "Today was my dad's first day at a day program, and I'm really worried it didn't go to well." My throat got tight. "But I don't know what my mom's going to do when I'm gone if she can't ever get a break."

I scratched Heidi's fur as I watched the waves roll in, then I looked at her sweet golden face. "Want to try a short walk by the water?"

She jumped, giving me all the answer I needed.

I stood back up, taking her leash and walking farther down the shore. Every so often, the waves lapped over my feet, giving me a refreshing jolt. With the sun shining on my skin and Heidi actually walking beside me, I felt hopeful.

I just hoped Dad had a good day at the center.

Now and then, Heidi would get distracted by a seagull or a crab, and I'd use Harini's tip of getting

Sadie's attention again by turning and calling her name.

At the end of our hour, I walked her back to Jesse. And when I say that man smiled big when I told him that she'd behaved so well... It made me so happy.

But even with the progress I'd made with Heidi, more nerves settled in as I walked home. Mom should be back with Dad by now. What if the day had been too much for him? What if it made things worse?

I approached our house, seeing Mom's car in the driveway next to mine. They were back.

I tried deep breathing to calm my nerves, counting backwards from ten, but my hand was still shaking as I turned the handle on the front door.

Every muscle in my body tensed as I braced myself for the worst.

Instead... I found my mom and dad on the couch while one of their favorite movies played on TV, *The Switch* with Jennifer Anniston and Jason Bateman.

The show was like a melody to my ears, relieving my anxiety so much I could cry.

Mom patted the couch next to her. "Want to come watch with us?"

I nodded, walking to the couch and curling under her arm just as Heidi had done to me earlier.

"How was your day?" Mom asked.

I thought back over the events, from arriving to school to walking with Heidi and then making sure a teacher found Diego and his friends without telling on him directly. A small smile tipped my lips as I said, "Alarmingly good."

SIXTEEN
DIEGO

JANICE SAID, "We have a lot to cover today, so please get settled in and take out your workbooks."

In less than a minute, she began covering professional communication skills. There was so much to consider that I'd never even thought of. How in retirement communities, these people had gone from living independently in their own homes for years to downsizing into a single room, sometimes shared with another person.

My gut ached at the thought of *Abuelita* or *Abuelo* having to do the same and some lame kid coming in and treating them like a chore. They deserved better than that.

There was more to the unit too, about how to communicate with patient families, charge nurses, housekeepers, and other people we might find in a residential or hospital setting.

As the class time neared its end, Janice said, "Don't get me wrong; the physical parts of care are important. Our people deserve to be safe, clean, well-fed, given their medications on a regular basis, but you CNAs... You're the ones who interact with them most. Sometimes more often than their own families."

That last sentence settled heavily over the room.

"Because of how important this is, I'm assigning you each partners to practice ten common conversations you'll have with your patients. You'll practice one conversation each week, record it, and submit it online."

A student up front cleared her throat. "Can we opt to do it alone?"

Raising her eyebrows, Janice said, "This is an important part of the job, and we don't have the time to do it in class. But I trust you'll exchange numbers and find something that works for you both."

Susannah's shoulders visibly sank.

And mine did too, because Janice said she was assigning us partners. That never worked in anyone's favor.

Janice began reading off the groupings. When she reached my name, I crossed my fingers under the table. *Someone good. Please someone good.*

"Diego, you'll be with April."

"Great," I said.

Everyone in class looked at me, and I realized I'd said it out loud, but my tone was worse than the word. My stomach sank. Now I was the one who looked like a jerk.

Janice stared me down like I was some naughty kid. "You'll have to work with all personality types, Mr. De Leon. I'm sure you and Miss Adams can manage to be together an hour a week."

We'd been together less than an hour since I met her, and she already hated my guts. Imagine what level of distaste I could accomplish with ten hours at my disposal.

Janice glanced at her watch. "That's time. I'll see you all next week. This week's communication project must be submitted by Thursday at midnight."

Everyone began packing up their bags, and I tried to make eye contact with April to indicate that we should talk, but she was already getting out of her seat, hurrying toward the door.

If she thought she was going to dodge me and

leave me with a bad grade on this, all for some dumb grudge... I grabbed my book and my backpack, following her out to the parking lot and rushing to stand between her and her driver's door.

"Diego!" she hissed. "Get out of the way."

"Whoa, I just wanted to make sure we're set for this project. This isn't exactly a class I can afford to slack in."

She folded her arms across her chest and stared at her door handle, like if she glared hard enough, she could get it to telepathically open and shove me out of the way.

"Look, I don't want to work with you either, but you heard Janice. She's not letting us out of this. So give me your number at least so we can set something up later, when you're not trying to bore a hole through my chest with your eyeballs."

"I don't have time for this," she said.

I raised my eyebrows. "You're making it take longer by arguing."

"No, I'm going to be late to pick up my dad." She stared at me impatiently. Probably seconds away from tapping her foot.

"Where is he, at dance lessons or something?"

Hurt flickered across her face, just long enough to make me wonder if that's actually where he was.

"Look, I didn't mean to be rude. I just... Can I have your number?" I stepped out of the way just to prove I wasn't a complete jerk.

She took the opportunity to get in her car. "Where will you be later?"

"The football game."

"See you then." Then she drove away.

I watched her car retreat, surprised April said she was coming to the game.

And as I made my way to my own car, a foreign feeling settled over my stomach. Something close to stomach upset, but not quite.

What the heck was going on with me? I had a game to play tonight and no time for whatever weird feeling this was.

I got into my car and dialed my older sister's number, letting the ringing sound from the speakers fill my car.

"I was just about to call you!" Des answered.

Backing out of the parking lot, I replied, "You were?"

"I wanted to wish you good luck for the game tonight. Last first game ever. I can't believe I won't be there cheering you on."

The feeling in my stomach intensified. "That's

kind of what I'm calling you about. I feel weird. I've never felt this way before a game."

"Weird? What do you mean?"

"Like my stomach's all in knots. It's like being nervous, but I have no idea why I would be." I looked both ways before continuing after the stop sign. "I've never been nervous before a game."

"You are Mr. Cool, Calm, and Collected. It's kind of annoying actually."

"Gee thanks." I continued toward the school, the feeling only growing.

"What happened earlier today? Did something bad happen at school?"

I wracked my brain, quickly settling on the last five minutes. "Well, I found out I'm homework partners with this girl who hates my guts."

"Someone hates you?" She sounded more surprised than me telling her I was nervous.

I rolled my eyes, even though she couldn't see me. "Her dog mauled me while I was surfing, and I told her to keep a hold of its leash before she hurts someone."

"Fair," Des said.

"But apparently that makes me public enemy number one."

"Okay, so you don't like her either."

I let out a sigh, focusing on the road as I got closer to the school. "She's annoying."

"It's the hesitation for me," she said.

"What does that mean? Are you saying she isn't annoying?" I reached the school parking lot and parked by Xander's truck.

"You've seen enough of Mom's telenovelas to know there's a fine line between love and hate."

I was really beginning to wonder why I called Des. "My life isn't a soap opera."

"Is she pretty?"

I sputtered. "Are you crazy?"

I could hear the smile in her voice as she said, "Is there any chance this 'stomach pain' is actually nerves because she's coming to your game."

"I'm hanging up now," I said.

She lowered her voice. "You want the truth? You can't handle the truth!"

"I'm calling Jude next time," I retorted and hung up the phone.

But as I got out of the car and started toward the locker room, I had one thought on my mind...

What if my sister was right?

MY HEART BEAT quickly as I drove away from ETC to the day center to pick up my dad. He'd had a decent first week, even though Wednesday night he was tired and went to bed earlier than normal. I assumed pick up would be okay.

But the thought of going to Diego's football game had me on edge. Sports and I did not get along, and sitting on a cold metal bleacher watching my enemy and a bunch of guys I barely knew did not sound like a fun time.

I pressed at the buttons on my dash to dial Sadie's number. She answered after a couple rings, saying, "My hands are covered in clay. You're on speaker phone."

"Any interest in going to a football game?"

Her mom squealed. "She'd love to go with you, April!"

Sadie let out a sigh. "Suddenly I've become great at ventriloquism."

Arlo's laughter boomed across the speaker, making me miss my dad's laugh even more. "You two should go, have fun. If only for the story."

"The story?" I asked.

Arlo replied, "When you're old like me, I want you girls to have stories to tell and not regrets to warn against."

I had a regret, alright, but it more so involved the fact that I'd have to see Diego tonight. He might have been the one to voice his disappointment in partner choice, but I was thinking the exact same thing.

I'd rather pair with the guy in the row in front of me who clearly had his headphones in throughout the entire lecture than spend an hour or more a week with Diego.

"I have to go tonight to talk to Diego about a class project," I explained. "You'd be doing me a real solid."

Another sigh. "Okay, I'll see you there."

We hung up, and I drove the rest of the way to

the center. I was just on time as I hurried to the front entrance, jamming my finger into the buzzer.

"How can I help you?" came a woman's voice.

"I'm April Adams. Here to pick up Doug Adams."

"Great. Come inside and wait in the lobby, please. Dr. Sanders wants to speak with you."

I squinted as the door unlocked, trying to figure out why Dad's doctor would want to talk to me as I pushed my way inside. But since no doctor was here, I had no choice but to wait. I hadn't taken the time to notice the waiting room earlier, but now I took it in. From the gold and red carpet underfoot to the beige chairs lining the walls, it was... okay. Not comfortable, not stylish, but not bad either.

I took a breath, getting a hint of eucalyptus mixed with cleaning solution.

"April?"

I looked up to see an older woman walking my way. She had on gray slacks, black clogs, a black shirt.

"I'm Dr. Sanders," she said, extending her hand.

"April," I replied, meeting her soft blue eyes framed by glasses.

There was a kindness in them as she looked me over. "Come with me, dear."

I followed her, looking around to see if I could catch a glimpse of my dad. For the last few days, he'd come home in a decent mood but way more tired than usual. The social worker told Mom that it would take time for him to adjust, especially with all the new therapies they were doing with him.

She stopped halfway down the hallway in an office labeled Dr. Sanders. I stepped inside, noticing the heavy wooden furniture ornately decorated with carvings. She gestured at a gold seat across from her desk and sat down.

"Is everything okay with my dad?" I asked, worried she was going to tell me he wasn't right for the program. It may have been hard, but I'd also seen my mom relax for the first time in years. On Wednesday, she even picked me up from school just so we could go get ice cream together. No worries about what Dad would do at home or if he'd try cooking and forget to turn off the oven. Just her and me.

The accident had changed my dad, but in a lot of ways, it had taken my mom from me as well.

"Your dad is adjusting better than most," Dr.

Sanders answered. "I think this program is exactly what he needs. I wanted to speak with you because we do things differently at Rhodora. I'm sure when you were in Kansas, the care was focused primarily on your father while you and your mom received little support."

I didn't need to confirm. The moment we got that call about his injury, our whole lives had shifted. Mom and I were an afterthought to Dad's care, his appointments, therapies, and medications, because we had to be there for him to get the help he needed.

"We know, from personal experience and working so closely with these families, that caregiver health is vital to the health of our patients. If the caregivers are struggling, the patients struggle as well."

I studied her for a moment, from the serious look in her eyes to the veins showing on her laced hands atop her desk. I didn't know what she was accusing us of... or if she had seen through the strong family we tried to be. "What do you mean?" I finally asked.

She tucked a lock of gray hair behind her ear. "If his care is ever too much, too hard, the sacrifices you and your mother make may not be in his best service."

My heart hardened in my chest, froze to a block of ice, the chill spreading. "Where else would he go?"

She reached into her desk and pulled out a brochure.

### RHODORA ACRES

SUPPORTED LIVING FOR ADULTS WITH TBI,
ALZHEIMER'S, AND OTHER COGNITIVE CHALLENGES

My eyes grew hot, and the feeling of failure, of desperation and fear blended with the ice in my veins. "Why are you showing this to me? Shouldn't my mom be involved?"

"She has been informed of this option as well, but I think it's important for all caregivers to know. Because even though you are a child, both your parents have told me what a help you've been."

A tear slipped down my cheek, and I wiped it away. How must it feel for my dad, a war veteran, a grown man, to know his daughter is partially responsible for him?

"You and your mom make a great team—we

can all tell how loved your dad is. But you're a senior in high school, April. You and your mother both deserve to have all the information before you decide to spread your wings." She smiled slightly, then stood. "Let's go get your father."

## EIGHTEEN
## DIEGO

COACH RIPLEY PACED in front of the players in the locker room, giving us a pep talk for our first game of the season. His khaki pants bunched at the waist, his headphones hung around his neck, and his Emerson Drafters polo strained at his stomach.

But that man could incite a team.

By the end of his talk, I could feel my heart beating faster. The nerves mingling with excitement at a chance to play.

"Bring it in!" Coach said.

The guys around me yelled, whooped, cheered, as we brought our hands in a pile. My helmet hung at my fingertips by my side.

"Drafters on three," Coach yelled.

Greyson, the team captain, yelled, "One, two, three!"

The rest of us followed. "DRAFTERS!"

We jogged out of the locker room into the dimming night sky toward the football field. Stadium lights shined against the dark blue sky. People milled about the stands, the parking lot, filling as we ran out to the field. The cheerleaders held up a DRAFTERS sign that the team ripped through to the crowd's cheers.

Greyson led us through stretches and then the first catching drill. While I waited for my turn, I scanned the audience. I easily spotted my family in the front row. Adelita and Marisol held up a sign that said die while Mateo held a sign that said GO. Mom and Dad sat next to them, sipping from cups of cocoa.

Then movement and a flash of turquoise caught my eye a few rows up. Sadie slid down the bleachers to an empty seat, and behind her, April's curvy frame did the same. She had on a pair of leggings clinging to her hips and an oversized dark blue shirt on top. I found myself wishing the shirt was as tight as her leggings.

"Diego!" Greyson yelled, and I cursed myself

for getting distracted by a girl who couldn't stand me.

I ran the pattern, catching his spiral and then tossing it back to Isaac, the second-string quarterback. He threw the ball to Greyson, and I jogged to the back of the line, determined to focus on the warmup. On the game. On anything but the girl in the stands, despite the distinct feeling of her eyes on my back.

Time ticked down on the scoreboard until the game started. As we lined up for the first kick of the game, my veins pulsated with adrenaline. Blood flowed to my muscles, prepping me to move. Everything faded out of my mind except for the plays I was supposed to run, the openings on the field.

The ref signaled kickoff, and for a few moments, the football flew through the air—the calm before the hurricane. Cheers blended with the plastic crash of pads and helmets. The thud of bodies pummeled to the ground. The smell of sweat and Gatorade. The feel of cold water sprayed through my helmet opening during a time out.

Then the clock counted down to halftime, the score even on both sides of the board. Before the guys went inside, I jogged to the cheerleaders at centerfield where they were beginning their part of the halftime routine.

Kenzie flounced up to me, a feather quill painted on her right cheek and my number on her left. "Go time," she said with a grin.

I cradled my hands just like we'd practiced, and she stepped in. Two other girls on the squad stood behind us and one in front as I flung her into the air. She spiraled and flipped before falling into my arms.

The crowd went wild, and I couldn't help but grin as she went back to the routine and I jogged to join the rest of my team.

"Showoff," Coach Ripley muttered with a smile, patting my back as I jogged by.

My grin only grew. I couldn't help it. What we players were doing on the field—it was challenging and fun. But all the people in the crowd? They were there for a show, and I was happy to give it to them.

Before we left the stadium, I glanced back to the stands, seeing April next to Sadie. I swore she was looking at me too before she glanced away.

We won the game, but barely. All of us guys were exhausted, but grinning ear to ear. Maybe it was just because I was a senior, but this win felt better than most.

Not least because of who I knew was in the audience.

And by that, I meant my family.

Of course.

They came down to the field, carrying the dieGO signs. Mom hugged me first. "*Mijo, serias increible.*"

"*Gracias,*" I replied, kissing her cheek.

"Yeah!" Mateo slapped a fist into his palm. "You pummeled that one guy right into the ground. I bet he still has turf in his face mask.

Dad chuckled and gave me a quick hug. "*Estoy orgulloso de ti, mijo.*"

My throat clogged every time he said it. "Thanks, Dad."

Marisol and Adelita told me good job as well, then Mom herded everyone away, saying, "We'll let you celebrate with your friends. See you later."

I waved and then more people congratulated me. Some guys on the team, a few freshmen girls with blushing cheeks. Kenzie and Deena, though they were more excited about the stunt we pulled off.

But April and Sadie didn't come by. I spotted them standing on the edge of the crowd, both looking uncomfortable and talking only to each other.

I extricated myself from the girls telling me good game and walked over to them. Sadie seemed surprised to see me walking toward them, but April's hazel eyes were dark as she traced my every step.

Sadie looked between the two of us, a small smile on her narrow lips. "Good game, Diego."

"Thanks," I said, my eyes still caught on April. The blue shirt wasn't an Emerson shirt—it had the Air Force logo on it. It was like a subtle slight to remind me *I'm not cheering for you*.

"Nice shirt," I said to April.

She folded her arms over her chest, covering the design. "I just came for your phone number."

I couldn't help but smirk. "The line was back there."

She made a disgusted sound and turned to leave, muttering something about failing the class being better than this.

"I'm joking," I said, "although I wouldn't expect

you to catch a joke. That would require a sense of humor."

She leveled a glare at me, while Sadie looked amused. Fair. April was really cute when she was mad at me.

"Do you have your phone?" I asked. "Or am I supposed to send a smoke signal with my number?"

April got it out of her leggings pocket.

"Hand it over. I'll type it in." I extended my hand, palm up.

"As if I'd trust you to come anywhere near my phone. Tell me your number and I'll text you."

I raised my eyebrows. "As if I'd trust you to text me."

Sadie shifted awkwardly foot to foot.

April wasn't budging.

"Diego," Xander called, jogging up to us. "We're going to Waldo's. You coming?"

"Give me a second," I told him, still eyeing April.

She groaned, passing me her phone. "Just get it over with."

I filled out the open contact form with my info and then sent myself a text before giving her phone back. "We should meet Sunday to work on the project," I said, running my fingers through my still damp hair. "Get it out of the way."

She shifted her hips, drawing my eyes away from hers. They were almost gold in the stadium lights. "Why not tomorrow? The sooner the better."

"My sister has dance on Saturday, and then I have to work. Nine on Sunday. I'll come to your place."

Her eyes widened quickly, and her shoulders tensed. "We can't do it at my house. The public library should be fine."

I scoffed. "Thought you wouldn't want to be seen with me. Just come to my house." I didn't want to give up good surfing weather for commuting across town. And my mom always made the best snacks when we had to study. But I wouldn't tell April I was only motivated by food and surfing.

She opened her mouth to argue, but I turned to catch up with Xander. "You know the address," I called over my shoulder. "Or at least your dog does."

## NINETEEN
## APRIL

JESSE ASKED me to walk Heidi Sunday, so I went to his place in the morning before going to study at Diego's house. Heidi and I practiced our turns, and she was much quicker to follow my lead this time. When I felt confident she'd stick by my side, we continued on our longer walk. She paraded beside me on the empty beach as waves rolled up to our feet. It was cool in the morning as little dots of salt-water hit my skin.

The smell, a mix of salt and fish and sun, was heavenly. Even if the humidity had my hair doing wild things.

"Heidi, wait," I said.

She tipped her head back toward me, the little

dot of dark brown fur above her golden-brown eyes lifting. Like she was asking me, *are you serious?*

"It won't kill you to stand still for a second," I said, holding her leash between my legs. I never would have done this a couple weeks ago, but she'd been doing so well lately. I pulled the band from around my wrist and lifted the waves from my neck, pulling it all up into a bun.

A seagull swooped by, and Heidi ripped her leash from my legs, happily chasing it.

"Heidi!" I shouted, finishing my bun as I ran after her. I came close to her and stepped on the leash, but my heel got caught in the loop and she pulled me completely over, landing my back in the sand.

"Stop!" I yelled, thankful the beach was empty this morning. If anyone had seen me, I'd bury myself in the sand right now.

My cheeks were hot regardless, as I got up and chased her down the beach. In the direction of Diego's house.

"Heidi, come back!" I called, hoofing it to the hard-packed sand so I could go faster. Running and I were not friends, but I'd be besties with running if it meant avoiding another run-in with Diego.

His house came closer, the one with a big glass deck and light gray walls.

"Heidi! TREAT!" I yelled, hoping no one would come out on the back porch. And by no one, I meant him. Please not Diego.

But then she romped into the water, acting like she could bite the waves to keep them from coming, and I breathed a sigh of relief, until I saw someone swimming back in on the white, foamy wave. His powerful arms sliced through the water, bringing him closer to shore.

He rose from the water, standing knee-deep for only a moment before Heidi jumped up, putting her paws on his broad chest.

Surprised, he fell over, the water hitting his chest. Heidi happily licked his cheek, his neck, all while I huffed, thinking this scene felt way too familiar. I'd have to tell the Pfanstiels that I couldn't walk Heidi anymore. I'd be way too busy burying my head in the sand to ever face society with her at my side.

He laughed, sitting up in the water, the waves splashing around his strong torso, and patted her damp shoulders, her neck, her chin.

He looked from Heidi to me, and I braced myself for another lecture about how I was a risk to society. But instead, he smirked and said, "She knew you couldn't stay away."

I gaped, open mouth like the fish they were probably swimming with, and Heidi looked happily at me, as if to say, *I do good?*

*No. No, you did not do good, you traitorous dog,* I said to her telepathically. *No more treats for you.*

Diego got up from the water, droplets falling down the ridges of his abs to the v of his hips and down his legs. And I stared, just like I had when he'd walked toward me on the football field, his dark curls damp, his undershirt clinging to his muscles while he held his shoulder pads over his helmet, hanging on to the face mask with his fingers.

Maybe the most annoying thing about Diego, besides his distractingly good looks, was how easy he made everything look, from playing with his team on a football field to chatting with girls at a party and earning Heidi's unending love. Even that impromptu stunt at the football game with his cheerleader girlfriend had been impressive. No matter how much I hated to admit it.

He handed Heidi's soaked pink leash to me, and I said, "I'm sorry. This dog has a mind of her own." *One entirely separate from mine,* I didn't add. "I'll walk her back to her owners' house and be back in half an hour for our study session."

"Her owners? Do you mean your parents?"

I shook my head. "One of our neighbors."

"Sure it's your neighbors." He seemed unconvinced.

"It is!" I argued, rubbing my aching hip. If only I could soothe my wounded pride as easily.

"Prove it."

Frustrated, I reached for her collar to see the tag. "Look, it says Heidi and has a phone number that is not mine."

"Could be your mom's."

His smirk was so dang annoying. "You know what? Come along. Meet her owners."

His eyebrows drew together. "You want to spend more time with me than you have to?"

"Of course not," I said flatly.

He stroked his chin like he was an old man thinking over his order at a restaurant. "It's not a bad idea. You can't keep a hold of this dog, so there's no telling when you'll get back for our study session, and I'd rather have it out of the way so I can actually enjoy my day."

"You're a real Prince Charming," I said. "But I

assure you, I'm no Cinderella. I don't need your saving."

"You're obviously not Cinderella. The animals actually listened to her." He took the leash back and started walking up the beach. "This is the way you came from, right? You know, before that act of grace?"

I gaped after him, my cheeks flaming hot.

"Don't worry," he said with a grin. "I didn't have my phone on me for any footage. Unfortunately."

I rolled my eyes at him, trying not to be completely embarrassed. He slowed—Heidi staying at his side like the perfect angel—waiting for me to catch up. When I did, we walked silently toward the Pfanstiels, but not the comfortable kind of silence. In the charged kind that made me anxious. Should I say something? Apologize for being so testy with him? Ask him to apologize for our bad first meeting (and subsequent poor encounters)? I didn't do great with conflict—honestly, I usually let stuff roll off my back since I always moved.

When people didn't stay in your life long, it was easier to forget they hurt you. Forget them all together. Apologies only mattered when people stuck around long enough for a relationship to have ups and downs.

Luckily, the Pfanstiels' wasn't far from the De Leons'. "This is it," I said, stopping at the picket fence. Diego walked with me up the brick path to their bright yellow door.

Mrs. Pfanstiel answered the door in her church clothes, and Heidi barreled past her, the leash dragging over their travertine tiles.

"Thank you, April! How fun to walk the dog with a friend."

"We're not friends," I said quickly, making everything so awkward.

Diego nodded. "We're studying for a class together."

"What a great idea." A crashing sounded in a room behind her, and Mrs. Pfanstiel rolled her eyes. "Better handle that. See you tomorrow, April."

She was already yelling at Heidi before the door even shut. Diego turned toward me, humor glinting in his eyes. And despite myself, I smiled back.

We walked down the brick path, our shoulders brushing as we passed through the gate. The amount of heat I felt on my skin from that one little touch made me want to dive in the ocean. Or at least get some distance. "I need to get my things from home. I'll see you in a little bit?"

"Where's your house?" he asked. "Should I walk with you to make sure you don't skip town?"

"The idea of skipping town is a good one, but I want to pass this class. I'll be at your place in fifteen minutes."

He hesitated, but eventually nodded. "I'll be on the back patio, if you want to walk on the beach instead of the road."

My heart constricted. It seemed like a thoughtful idea, but that didn't line up with what I knew of Diego.

He waved goodbye and walked down the beach, and I had to wonder... How well did I really know my enemy?

I COULD SEE April walking back up the beach toward my family's house. She had on shorts and a loose shirt that whipped around her curves in the wind. This far away, she couldn't see me well enough to tell I was staring. So I stared, and I asked myself, *what was it about this girl who caught my eye and demanded my attention?*

Why was it so hard to look away? I had never been this shallow in my life.

She came closer, and I got up from the patio table to straighten the cushions, ready my book, act like I hadn't been staring at the way her hips swayed as she walked.

Sand swished under her feet as she got near, and

her breaths punctuated the waves. "Let's get this over with," she huffed, pulling a string bag from her back.

"Great attitude," I replied, trying not to smile.

Ignoring me, she set her canvas bag on the glass tabletop and loosed the drawstring. She pulled out our book and a notebook with a pen. Then she pulled out a chair and settled into the seat.

A breeze kicked up strands of hair from her ponytail, swirling them around her face. The contrast of the dark brown locks against her fair skin was stunning.

She looked up from her notebook, catching me staring, and gave me an annoyed look like I was moving way too slowly.

I got into my own chair, opening my notebook to my notes on the assignment. "We're supposed to practice a conversation with a patient who is telling us about their late spouse."

A shadow crossed April's face, just as visible as her arched eyebrows or her full pink lips. "Why is she having us do this?" she murmured, almost to herself.

Trying—and failing—to understand her expression, I looked back at my notes. "One of us has to role-play the patient and the other has to role-play the CNA."

"I'll be the patient," she offered.

"Cool." I was about to ask her if she just wanted to improv the conversation, but the back patio door slid open, and my mom came out, holding a tray of food. Mateo came out behind her with a sloshing pitcher of juice and two cups.

Mom smiled at us. "Can't have a study session without snacks."

April's lips parted. She seemed... surprised.

I helped Mateo get the pitcher on the table without dumping it in April's lap, and Mom put the small charcuterie board between us. She'd even used olives to spell CNA between all the fruit, meat, cheese, and crackers.

"Thanks," I said, getting up to kiss her cheek.

She put her arm around my waist. "You need brain food to do well in school." Mom smiled at April. "Hi there. I'm Diego's mom. Everyone calls me Mama De."

April gave my mom the most genuine smile I'd ever seen her wear. "This is amazing, really."

*And a compliment?*

Why was I jealous of my mom?

And why was my heart picking up speed?

"Oh, honey, it's no big deal," Mom said. "I want all of Diego's friends to feel welcome here."

I glanced at April to see how she reacted to my mom calling her a friend. Her shoulders stiffened slightly, her chest rising.

*Ouch.*

Mom added, "Even friends who got off to a rough start." She winked at April. "It takes boys a while to learn, but they do eventually."

April smiled back at my mom, her cheeks slightly pink. "He told you about that?"

Mom said, "No matter how old children get, they always need their mom."

Mateo whined, "Mom, can we go to *Abuelita's* now?"

Mom ruffled his hair, silky straight like Dad's instead of curly like mine and Mom's. "Yes, we can. You two have fun. And April, you're welcome back any time, okay? We'll treat you just like family."

"Thank you," April said, her voice almost a whisper.

Mom and Mateo walked back through the patio door, and I reached for the cups, pouring both of us some juice. When I looked up from the cups, I noticed April wipe at her eyes.

My gut clenched, and my muscles tightened,

like I could fight whatever invisible force had caused her to cry. "Are you okay?" I asked.

She nodded, looking up at me. Her hazel eyes were bright now, almost golden green. "I just hadn't expected her to make this feel like home... after everything between us."

"Mama De's heart for kids is bigger than the ocean. And she'll go full-blown mama bear against any adult who tries to cross one of us kids."

"Yeah?" April sniffed.

"Last year, this agent hurt my sister's feelings, and we called her *la bruja,* the witch, for an entire year."

Her smile didn't seem so forced this time. "It means a lot."

I examined her for a moment. She hadn't wanted me to study at her place. My mom bringing snacks brought her to actual tears. My stomach turned at the thought that she didn't have a good homelife. But I didn't know her well enough to ask —just well enough to know she'd never tell me if I did.

"Let's get to it," April said. "I think we can come up with a few talking points and then wing it from there."

For the next half hour, we snacked and worked

on the assignment. Amicably. April came up with a few good points and even told me good job on one of my ideas. It meant far more than it should have.

Then I set up my phone against the pitcher, and we filmed ourselves having the conversation.

It was the longest I'd ever looked at April without resorting to sneaking glances. Her eyes were the most interesting part of her, the way the colors starburst around her pupils. And then her lips. She bit her bottom lip when she was thinking, making the color deepen from light pink to a deep plum, and it took all I had not to reach up and free her abused bottom lip from her white teeth.

When we finished with the video, she flipped through the assignment, and I noticed three dark blue dots on her right hand, underneath the pinky knuckle. They were almost imperceptible, blending with the few freckles she had on her skin.

"What is that?" I asked, brushing the back of her hand.

Her skin was hot under mine, and she pulled back like I'd shocked her. Holding her hand in her other, she rolled it over, examining the dots, a small smile on her face. She pulled that bottom lip between her teeth again, and I stared.

"It was a bet with these kids at my last school. A stick-and-poke tattoo—they didn't say where."

"What did you win?"

"Twenty bucks—and a week of grounding." She laughed slightly, still looking down at her hand. "Not for getting a tattoo, but for giving in to peer pressure."

I chuckled at her little act of rebellion, the smile it brought to her lips. "Where was your last school?"

"Junction City, Kansas."

"Kansas?"

She nodded. "My dad was stationed near there at Fort Riley."

"He's in the military?"

"Was," she clarified. Her jaw clenched, but her voice stayed even as she said, "Army. He was injured on his last deployment. Medically discharged from the service three years ago."

The pieces of her story locked into place, making so much sense. "So the person you know with a brain injury..."

She nodded, staring down at her hand for a moment longer before reaching for her book and putting it in her bag.

"I'm... sorry," I said, but it sounded so flat. So inadequate compared to the truth she'd admitted.

Her dad had been injured in the service. She had needed a nurse's kindness. She had been leaving ETC to pick him up. He couldn't drive. I couldn't go to her house.

I looked up to say something more, but she was already gone.

DAD DIDN'T WANT to go to the center on Monday. Dr. Sanders said to give him a day off since it's a big adjustment, and I could see the way my mom deflated. Instead of going out and working and not having to worry about anyone but herself, for a few hours at least, she was back in our home.

The brochure I kept in my backpack felt like a weight growing heavier by the day.

On Tuesday, he refused to go to the center and broke all the picture frames in the living room, including the last family photo we took before his injury.

On Wednesday, Dr. Sanders sent a pickup for

him. Two men escorted him to the van as Mom and I held each other and cried.

I stayed home from school that day.

The next day I went only because I'd already missed two days of school and we were just a few weeks in. By noon Friday, I felt like I'd had the longest week of my life, and I still had my CNA class to go to.

I walked into the classroom and took my usual seat, getting my materials ready along with everyone else. When it was time for class to start, Janice began speaking. "You all did great work on this last project, but one pair of students did exceptionally well. I'll play their video for you all to see exactly what I'm looking for next week."

She tapped on her computer, and her screen reflected on the whiteboard through the projector. She tapped a file, and Diego and I appeared larger than life.

We sat next to each other, all our differences on stark display. He was so fit, so strong, with his muscles straining against his T-shirt sleeves and his perfect bone structure on full display. I sat next to him, my shoulders sloping and my double chin visible. My hair drawn back in a ponytail looked messy and frizzy compared to his dark curls. His skin was a beautiful golden tan while mine was practically reflective.

We began speaking on the screen, his voice low and clear as he pretended to be a CNA. We had a few-minutes long conversation, falling into our roles, and then the video came to an end.

Janice clapped, leading everyone else in the class to do the same. "Very good job, you two. Don't know what there was to worry about."

I chanced a glance at Diego and found him looking right back at me. I quickly averted my gaze, but not before I saw him smile.

As the clapping died down, Janice said, "Everybody up."

I looked around the room, confused. A college student up front asked, "Are we getting out early?"

Janice chuckled. "Wishful thinking, my dear. We have a project, and it's hands-on."

We all got up, leaving our bags in the classroom, and followed Janice down the hallway until we reached a big cafeteria, not too different from the one at Emerson Academy. Most of the round tables were empty, except for two loaded with trays of food.

"Gather 'round," Janice said to us. "We're going to be practicing feeding today. One of the most important skills you'll learn. Food is life, and making this an enjoyable experience for those you work with can enrich their lives greatly. Get two trays and sit at a table beside your homework partner."

I immediately felt Diego's eyes on me. It had been a long week, and sitting across from him for the rest of class was the last thing I wanted to do. But the only way out was through, so I got my tray and met him at a round table.

We had it to ourselves, and I looked anywhere other than at him. Eventually my eyes landed on the food. It actually looked good—mashed potatoes, corn, applesauce, and meatloaf with what looked like barbecue sauce.

One of the students passed out a print off from our textbook while Janice stood toward the front of the cafeteria, going over feeding and the process we would have to follow. It was more intricate than I ever thought, and in the back of my mind, I wondered if this was how it would be for Dad if he lived at the Rhodora. If his care would be this thoughtful.

"Ready?" Diego asked.

I almost didn't realize Janice had finished her lesson. "Sure. Do you want to practice first?"

"Sure," he said, looking down at his sheet. "Would you like a clothing protector, Adams?"

I nodded. Diego was not ruining my uniform with this barbecue sauce.

"Good call." He got up, going to the tub Janice had on a table. He came back to me and said, "Okay if I put it on you now?"

"Sure," I replied.

For how strong Diego was, he was equally as gentle, slipping the material over my head, brushing my hair out of my face, and then straightening the fabric so it rested smoothly over me.

Why did the simple act almost bring tears to my eyes?

Luckily, he didn't notice, already looking back to his sheet. "Do you want tea or water today?"

"Water is fine," I said. "With ice."

Nodding, he got up and retrieved a cup. Without his blazer on, I could see his muscles move under his pale blue uniform shirt. If he ever worked in a retirement home, those ladies would be all over him.

"What are you smiling about?" he asked as he walked back.

"Nothing," I said quickly. "Thank you for the water."

"You're very polite today."

"Maybe because I don't want a spoon to the back of the throat."

He rolled his eyes at me, which only made me smile more. "What would you like to eat first, Adams?"

"Mashed potatoes?" I said.

Janice called out, "Remember to correct posture! Even if it feels uncomfortable, it's massively important. Sitting incorrectly is a big choking hazard."

"Can you please sit up?" he asked me.

I shifted in my seat, doing as he asked.

He glanced at the paper again, then filled the spoon half full, just like Janice had told him. His eyebrows were drawn slightly together, focus in his eyes. And for a guy who never took anything seriously, it was endearing to watch him try like this. Too endearing.

I needed to focus on something else.

Like the mashed potatoes coming toward my face.

I opened my mouth, taking a bite of the salty dish, and swallowed.

"Good?" he asked.

I nodded.

Janice called out, "This room is too quiet! Remember, dinner is a social activity! You need to speak to each other."

Diego filled his spoon halfway. "How about them Badgers."

"Like the animal?" I asked. But the spoon was too close to my face, and he laughed, making his arm move and missing my mouth completely.

"Diego!" I cried, wiping at my face.

"Sorry, sorry." He reached for a napkin, still laughing. "Let me."

I wanted to argue, but Janice had said we needed to practice this. His face was close to mine; I could smell the gum on his breath as he wiped away the potatoes. "The Badgers are a professional football team in Brentwood. Just twenty minutes from here. Haven't you heard of them?"

"Your game was the first football game I've ever watched," I admitted. "And don't be too proud of yourself. I was there for the sake of the class."

"For the class," he repeated, a smirk on his lips. "Would you like a drink?"

I nodded, letting him lift the cup to my lips, angling the straw to my mouth. I felt his eyes on me as I sucked.

My cheeks heated beyond measure.

Diego cleared his throat. "So we can't talk about football. What about the Academy? Are you liking it?"

I bit my lip as he filled the spoon half full with potatoes. "You mean besides the obnoxious guy in first hour?"

His eyes practically gleamed. "Besides him." He pressed the food to my mouth and I ate it, slowly feeling my defenses melting away.

"It's not so bad."

Now he smiled. "Good."

Janice yelled out that it was time to switch, and I made sure to get on even footing, dabbing mashed potatoes on his nose.

He laughed like a good sport, and then I brushed the food away from his flawless tan skin.

We talked about school, and he told me a little bit more about football until it was time for us to clean up.

After class, we made plans to meet for our assignment and began walking different directions. But before he reached his car, I said, "Diego?"

He turned, facing me again, the light catching his eyes just right to make them a pretty amber color. "Yeah?"

I was so distracted by his eyes I almost forgot

what I was going to say. "Um, good luck at the game tonight." According to the announcement over the PA system, it would be at a town about an hour away and a fairly even matchup.

His eyes crinkled slightly with his smile. "Thanks, April. Don't know how I'll play without you glaring at me from the stands."

I rolled my eyes. "I'm sure you'll deal just fine."

His smile twisted to the side, and he nodded, turning back toward his car.

## TWENTY-TWO

## APRIL

THE NEXT MORNING, Mom brought coffee to my room, waking me up.

I rubbed at my eyes as I sat up. "What are you doing awake?" I glanced at my clock, showing the time was just a little past seven. "Aren't Saturdays for sleeping in?"

Her eyes glimmered way too much for it to be this early. "I have other plans."

"What do you mean?"

She took a sip of her coffee, smiling all the while. "Since we're living in California, I thought it was important for you to start taking part in the culture."

"You mean by saying *bruh* and walking around

in my swimsuit?" I teased. Maybe I was being a little salty, since the coffee hadn't kicked in yet.

Her laugh filled the room. "No, I signed you up for surf lessons."

I stared at her face, looking for a hint of a joke in her pale blue eyes. Unfortunately, I didn't find one. "Mom. I do not do sports."

"You only hit that instructor with your racket one time," Mom argued.

I shuddered. "You're not the one who got kicked out of tennis lessons while everyone watched." It wasn't my fault I didn't understand what a backhand swing meant.

"The instructor assured me that this would be very low pressure and that people of all abilities do just fine. Besides, it's only ninety minutes. You can do anything for an hour and a half."

"Like completely embarrass myself in front of some poor, unsuspecting soul?" I asked.

"Oh please." She batted her hand at me like I was being silly. "Surf instructors see it all, I'm sure."

"Okay, but what if I drown? I'm decent at best in water *without* waves."

"Already asked—he said you wouldn't go out deeper than you could touch."

I pressed my lips together, slightly annoyed that Mom had thought of it all.

"If you hate it, you can tell me all about it over s'mores later."

That perked me up. "S'mores?"

She nodded. "There's a gas fire pit being delivered later, along with a grocery order. I thought it could be a fun way for us to spend the evening."

I let out a sigh. She'd used my weakness against me. But she was right. I could do anything for ninety minutes. The last few years had shown me that.

And who knew? Maybe I'd meet some hot surf instructor and get some nice eye candy for a couple hours. It couldn't be that bad.

## TWENTY-THREE

I WAS WRONG.

So freaking wrong.

We'd only driven two minutes before Mom parked in front of a house I recognized and glanced at the GPS on her car's screen. (She'd insisted on taking me so I wouldn't back out of the lessons. She knew me too well.) "The instructor said you could meet him back behind this house."

"Mom?"

"Yes?"

I turned away from the house and looked at her. "Do you know the instructor's name, by chance?"

"Yes! It's Diego—Marcy Pfanstiel just *raved* about him teaching her granddaughter to surf a couple years back. I think he's close to your age."

She had no idea.

And then she had the audacity to wink. "Maybe there's a cute surfer boy romance in your future."

I stared at her, horrified. "Mom, Diego is—"

Her eyebrows raised. "You know him?"

"We go to school together. He's..."

Satan's spawn?

But that wasn't true because his mom had been so kind to me, it almost brought me to tears.

"Not interested in me," I said finally. "He always has some skinny blond girl hanging off his arm."

Mom shook her head. "Sometimes boys will surprise you."

Diego had been nothing but a surprise—from his rude first impression to his thoughtful answers in our CNA class project. I bit my lip, worried about how he would surprise me today. What version of him would I get? The guy who'd yelled at me my first day here or the one who was decently nice spoon-feeding me mashed potatoes?

"You can do this," Mom said, patting my arm. "I can't wait to hear how it goes."

That was the sign, her gentle goodbye because she needed to get back to the house in case Dad woke up and needed something.

"I'll see you later," I replied, getting out of the car. I reached into the back seat for my beach bag with my beach towel, a water bottle, and sunscreen in case I decided on a second application.

Knowing I was walking toward Diego, I suddenly felt more self-conscious. I'd already embarrassed myself in front of him—mostly because of Heidi. This time, any embarrassment would be all me. And I didn't like the thought of that.

Mom's engine revved softly as she drove away, and I continued down the path that went between the two houses, toward the beach. It was a beautiful day—a soft breeze, warm sunshine, and perfectly blue skies with white puffy clouds. The ocean waves crashed, one after another, toward the light brown sandy shore.

Then I saw him, sitting beside two surfboards in the sand. One board lay flat, blue and white, and the other next to it bright orange. He had on dark red swim trunks, contrasting the pale sand. The way he bent over showcased the muscles of his back, shoulders. There was a dark purple bruise on his side. It worried me, until I remembered the football game the night before.

I didn't know how it went, if Emerson had won.

And for the first time, I found myself caring for the outcome of a sporting event.

He glanced over his shoulder, his eyes traveling over me and a frown growing on his face. "You?"

My chest constricted. We were back to this again. "I can go back home," I replied, wrapping my arms around my waist and wishing my mom hadn't bought me a rash guard that showed my stomach. Wishing she hadn't signed me up for this lesson.

"No," Diego said. "It's fine."

I watched him get up from the sand. "Fine?"

He nodded, then launched into an explanation of where to stand on the surfboard. He placed his feet atop the orange board, placing them square in the middle and explaining something about weight distribution and balance, but it all went over my head.

What was with the ice-out? I thought we had a decent conversation yesterday. And was it really that awful to *get paid* to teach me to surf? Because I knew he wouldn't do this for free.

He looked at me expectantly.

"Sorry, what?" I said.

"Step on the board."

My body was stiff as I placed my feet atop the surfboard, trying to copy what he'd done earlier.

His lips settled together as he gave my legs an assessing look, making me hyperaware that my swim shorts were already riding up, giving a great display of my thick thighs and cellulite. I pulled down at the fabric and waited.

He bent down, his hands inches from my foot. Thankfully I'd painted my toes the night before. "Mind if I..."

Yes, I minded. But I could do anything for ninety minutes. Including being guided by my enemy. "Go ahead."

His hands were warm on my calf as he guided my left foot forward and gently nudged my right foot so it was parallel to the other. "You want to keep a good center of gravity on the board. Otherwise, you'll change directions or fall."

Falling was inevitable as far as I was concerned. "I can barely keep my balance on even ground. With or without a dog."

He smirked. "Why don't you lie on the board?"

I watched him for a second. "Diego, we really don't have to do this. I know my mom thinks I can do anything, but if someone my size can't surf, I totally understand."

His eyebrows drew together, and he quickly shook his head. "Size has nothing to do with it." He counted on his fingers. "As long as you can do a push-up and move your feet on the board, you can surf. My sister Des is about your size, and she can hold her own on the waves."

Something snapped inside my mind, and I found myself choking on air. "Wait. Your sister's name is Des?"

He nodded.

"Like Des De Leon?" It was a miracle I was still upright.

Again, he nodded.

"The one dating *Jude Santiago*?"

That smirk was back. "So you're a Fantiago?"

My jaw dropped. "You're kidding. Tell me you're kidding."

"I'm kidding."

I hit his shoulder. "Diego! I thought you were related to a famous person."

"Watch it, killer." He laughed, grabbing his shoulder.

I shook my head. "I knew there was no way someone like you shared DNA with a goddess like Des De Leon"

He laughed. "Oh, I do. She's my sister."

My jaw dropped. He *had* to be kidding me. "How is that even possible?"

"I guess that's a question for the big guy. Although, Des did used to tell me I was adopted, but I think that's just something big sisters do." With a shrug, he nodded toward the board. "Now lie down on the board. We'll practice standing up."

## TWENTY-FOUR

## APRIL

FOR THE NEXT FIFTEEN MINUTES, I got up and down on my board so much, I thought he was messing with me. When I accused him of just trying to give me a workout, he said, "It's easier to practice on land than it is in the water. But I think you're ready to go if you want to."

I looked from my board on solid ground to the roiling waves. I wasn't letting Diego see how afraid I was. Even if I was terrified of getting dragged under the water and making a fool of myself.

The ocean was beautiful, but it was also strong, powerful...deadly.

"Ready?" Diego asked.

I nodded. Lies. All lies.

He bent, wrapping the surfboard leash around my ankle. My skin sizzled under his touch. I attributed it to the fact that I wasn't used to being touched. Any girl who'd never had a first kiss would have her hormones in a frenzy if a guy her age got close. I stayed still to show it didn't affect me, even though the burn stayed long after his fingers pulled away.

He carried the surfboard for me, his arms flexing powerfully as he lifted it. At the water's edge, he said, "Shuffle your feet when you get in the water. There are stingrays here sometimes."

My heart stalled. "Stingrays?"

He nodded.

And here I'd been worried about embarrassing myself. Now I had to contend with the thing that murdered Steve Irwin?

Seemingly oblivious to the fear racing through my veins, Diego led the way into the water. I followed behind, the chill hitting my skin as I shuffled my feet along the sandy bottom. Determined not to show any weakness, I stepped in up to my waist, focusing on the warm sun instead of the cold water.

A big wave crashed against me, flinging water up to my shoulders. I flinched, and Diego said,

"When a wave comes, it's best to hold your board like this." He swung it out to his side, so it was parallel to the waves. "If you put it in front of you, it'll smack you down—I've even seen people break their nose that way."

Later, when I was warm in front of the fire, eating s'mores, I'd tell my mom what a terrible idea this lesson had been. Between the risk of stingrays, jellyfish, drowning, and now broken bones, I didn't know why anyone went surfing at all.

In a break between the waves, he said, "Okay, climb on."

I looked at the board, put my hands on either side, and tried to pull myself up.

Tried.

Instead, the board flipped over, and I fell below the water, coming up sputtering. Completely humiliated, I said, "We can just go back to shore. I can't do this. I don't even know why I tried." I started walking back, ready to hide myself forever.

Diego reached for my hand, his face just a board's width distance from mine. "You can do this."

"Doubtful," I said just loud enough for him to hear.

"I'll hold the board," he said. He reached

across, hanging on to both sides. "Lift yourself so your body's parallel to the board before trying to get on."

Just knowing this would end in disaster, I held on and kicked my legs and struggled... but Diego held the board steady. Finally, my stomach pressed against the board, but my weight shifted it from side to side, and I crashed under again.

Right as I came up, another wave crashed against us, tossing me under, and I came up sputtering again, panic rising in my veins. I didn't have panic attacks often—maybe one or two my entire life. But I felt one coming on, my vision growing tunneled.

Diego let go of the board, letting my leash keep it from flying back to shore, and he put his hands on my shoulders, leaving mere inches between us. "Breathe, April."

My name... He said my name.

"When you get nervous, your body tenses up, but the best thing to do is relax."

"Relax?" I repeated, my voice shrill. The last thing I could do with these waves hitting us was relax.

Another one came, and I jumped, desperately trying to keep my head above water.

"On the next one, we're going to swim under it," he said.

"Under?" He probably thought I was a parrot at this point, squawking panicked words back at him.

He nodded. "It's calmer down there. So when this wave comes, swim down."

I wanted to argue, but the water was already rolling toward us. I sucked in a breath and dove down, paddling furiously under the water. I wasn't sure if the wave was gone yet, but I came up, sucking in a desperate breath.

Diego came up next to me, water gliding down the planes of his face. "Good. Let's do it again."

"*Again?* I barely made it through that one!"

"This time see if you can touch the sand," he said evenly.

With the next wave coming, I didn't have time to argue and breathe. So I pulled in a breath and ducked under the water, paddling until my hands grazed the sand underneath. When I came up again, I saw Diego, nodding.

"Good. One more time."

I took another breath, determined to get better at this. Determined to face this fear. Determined to show Diego that whatever faith he had in me to keep doing this wasn't completely misplaced.

Another wave came, and I dove down. This time, as the wave rolled over us, I felt a gentle but firm tug on the leash at my ankle.

As I came up, I saw Diego's smile, just as gentle. Just as real as the pressure on my ankle had been. "Did you feel that?" he asked.

I nodded.

"I've got you, April," he said earnestly, holding my gaze. "I've got you."

Something in my heart twinged. Loosened. Became confused.

Why did those four words mean so much to me, coming from Diego no less?

"Let's try again," he said, bringing the board back between us.

Trying not to feel so nervous, I pulled myself up again.

He held the board, like he'd said, and then I was on it, my hands gripping the sides and my toes dangling over the edges to keep me on.

The board wobbled, and Diego said, "Hips to the right."

I tried to do what he asked, then I wobbled to the side again. "To the left!"

After a few more rounds, the board stabilized.

A wave rolled toward us, and he pointed me face first at the wave. I reared back, getting smacked in the face with salty water.

"Hang on to the board," he ordered.

"I'm trying not to drown," I hissed.

I swear I heard him chuckle.

If another wave wouldn't have been coming, I would have turned and given him a piece of my mind. Instead, I hung on like he asked, getting smacked again by the water.

"Can we turn around now?" I asked. This was *miserable*.

Without replying, he turned my board sideways. "You're going to ride this one. Once you get some speed, stand up. Remember to slide your feet to get in the right position."

The wave swelled under me, picking up the board and propelling me quickly back to the shore. The rush of the water blending with the speed of the wind over my face was... almost magical.

So magical I wasn't going to ruin it by standing up and falling off.

I rode the wave until the board slowed and I could step back into the water, careful not to land on any stingrays.

I turned to see Diego walking toward me, his abs rippling with each step through the water. *Why did he have to look so good?*

His lips stretched into a heart-melting grin. "That was great!" he said. "Now you know the feel of the board. Let's get on the beach and practice standing up again so you can do it next time."

Grateful for a break from the relentless waves, I bent to grab my board, but Diego quickly reached to carry it for me. "I've got it."

I unclipped the strap at my ankle, remembering the complete sense of comfort I'd felt when he tugged the leash and spoke those words.

I followed Diego back from the packed sand to the softer beach, each grain sticking to my wet feet and ankles.

"Okay, show me what you've got," he said by the board.

I did as he asked, but now that my shorts and rash guard were wet, they were riding up more than ever. I stood atop the board and pulled my shirt down so it showed less of my midriff and then tugged at my shorts.

Diego's voice was short as he said, "Try again."

I gave him a confused look. I thought we'd had

a moment together, but maybe I had been wrong. This hot and cold treatment from him was starting to give me whiplash.

Without saying a word, I lay in the middle of the board, then pushed up, putting my front leg in the center of the board and my back leg behind me.

"Remember, your feet need to be parallel," he said, a tinge of annoyance in his voice.

I let out a sigh and straightened up, pulling at my shorts again. I really needed to find a new swimsuit if I ever did this again.

"Again," he barked.

I gave him a look before bending over and lying flat on the board. Why was he pushing me so hard? It didn't even matter if I could do this or not. I was about a hundred percent sure that I was never surfing again unless I suddenly developed a taste for saltwater and humiliation.

With another breath, I pushed myself up, angling my feet like he said.

He was quiet, and I glanced up under my eyelashes, ready for the next snappy command.

"Better," he said gruffly.

I readjusted my legs from the stance and adjusted my shorts again.

His hand covered mine, resting right above my thigh. His voice was husky as he said, "If you keep covering those beautiful thighs, I'm going to lose my mind."

## TWENTY-FIVE

## DIEGO

HER WIDE OCEAN eyes landed on mine, searching for an explanation.

The problem?

I had none. My hand was still over her hand, touching the soft skin of her thighs, covering her cute little stick-and-poke tattoo, and I couldn't move. How did I tell her that her body was beautiful and that the way she fussed over it only made looking away that much more difficult?

I'd had a horrible time at the party when she was in those lacy shorts, trying to keep my eyes off her legs, but now, with the water sliding down her curves and her brown hair almost black as it framed her pale face... She was a siren. A song I couldn't ignore.

She caught her bottom lip between her teeth, toying with me more. She had to be doing this on purpose. And if she wasn't? She had power she didn't know how to handle, and I didn't either.

"Diego," she breathed.

Her voice snapped me out of my response, and I pulled away. "You should wear a wet suit next time. The water's cold."

Her lips parted, drawing my gaze again. "That's not what you said."

I knew what I said.

And I couldn't take it back.

"Say it again," she breathed.

My stomach muscles clenched, and I couldn't stop thinking about her lips. Those full lips. Just like her thighs. Curvaceous. Voluptuous. Everything I liked.

"I said..." I closed the gap between us, smelling her shampoo, the sharp ginger scent mingling with the saltwater in her hair. "If you keep covering those beautiful thighs, I'm going to lose my mind."

Her lips parted, like they wanted me to pay attention. "Beautiful?"

I nodded sharply. She had to know how beautiful they were, right along with the rest of her.

"I thought..." She swallowed, her throat moving. "I thought you hated me."

My laugh came out like a bark. "I do. You're quick to judge, short with your words, glare like your life depends on it, and way too good at distracting me during class."

She lifted her chin, not shying away from me. "I don't like you either."

"Oh yeah?"

"You act like you own the beach. Walk around school like you expect everyone to adore you. And I'm still annoyed that Heidi actually listens to you."

My lips tipped up of their own accord. "So we agree. We don't like each other."

"Right." She tilted her head, her eyes tracking from mine to my mouth.

I stepped closer, seconds from discovering if her lips were actually as soft as they looked.

"DIEGO!" my brother Mateo yelled from the back patio.

April jumped away from me like she'd been tased. And we both looked toward my house in time to see Kenzie following my little brother outside.

"YOUR GIRLFRIEND'S HERE," Mateo shouted.

"She's not my girlfriend," I muttered, but it was

too late. That cold, distant look was back in April's eyes.

"I'm going home to change," she said. "I'll come back later to do the homework."

I allowed myself to watch, for just a few moments, as she walked away from me. She didn't look back.

With I sigh, I went back to the house, leaving the boards in the sand. Mateo had already gone back inside, and Kenzie was sitting on one of the patio chairs, tapping on her phone. She had her hair pulled into a high ponytail, looking like she'd been out for a run.

"What are you doing here?" I asked.

She gave me a surprised smile. "Whoa, killer."

"Sorry." I scratched my neck, dropping down into the chair across from her. "What's up?"

"I needed guy advice, and you're the first person I thought of."

I tried not to be annoyed that she came at the worst possible time. "Why do you need advice?"

Her cheeks pinked slightly. "You know the quarterback from Brentwood Academy?"

I scowled. He had the best arm in our division.

"That's the one," she said.

"You know him?"

She nodded. "He messaged me online about a week ago, and we've been talking nonstop." Her smile grew from tentative to excited. "He asked me on a date."

"Wow." I sat back in the chair. "I thought you didn't date since..."

"Phillip," she finished for me. She took a breath to steady herself. "I didn't think I wanted to either, but it's been a long time since freshman year. Maybe it would be good for me to move on, get some practice in before we leave for college." She studied her fingernails, a nervous habit of hers.

"Sounds like you have it figured out," I said.

She bit her lip, but it had nowhere near the effect on me that April did. "I'm going on a date with him tonight."

"Where are you going?" I asked. I swear if she was going to his house to 'watch a movie' I'd pummel him myself.

"Out to dinner at Viewhouse." She shimmied her shoulders, letting her happiness show. And I was happy for her, truly, but I couldn't get my mind off the way April's skin felt under my hand. How my mind had seemed to disappear, leaving unfiltered words pouring from my mouth.

Still, I smiled at Kenzie's enthusiasm. "That's a

good place for a first date. So what do you need advice for?"

She leaned forward, a serious look on her face. "*What if I like him?*"

I laughed. "Looks like I'll be going by myself to homecoming. What am I going to do without my wing woman?"

She rolled her eyes at me. "You know you could ask pretty much any girl in school and have a date in a heartbeat."

"That's exactly what I want. Some girl looking at me like I'm a piece of meat all night." I shook my head.

"Oh, Diego." She shook her head and looked like she was about to say something.

"What?" I asked.

She paused for a moment. "Is there a reason you're so afraid of dating? I mean, as far as I know, you've never had a bad heartbreak, your parents are totally fine with you going out. And there's not a lack of girls who'd be interested…"

I eyed her suspiciously. "I thought *you* were the one who wanted advice."

"Well, I just want you to know, if you're, you know, not interested in women, that's okay with me. I'd love you either way."

"Good grief," I muttered, getting up and walking toward the beach.

She had the audacity to follow. "What is it then?" she demanded.

I stopped in the sand, facing her. "You want know what it is?"

She nodded, impatiently putting her hands on her hips. "Tell me."

"I saw my older sister's heart get broken by that jerk she dated. I watched my guy friends turn into someone completely different the second a girl got involved. There's never been someone who's worth the risk."

She toed the sand thoughtfully. "You know, it's been nice talking to someone who likes me that way. Maybe you would think it was nice too. Possibly with a girl you keep staring at when you think no one's looking... if it's worth the risk." She winked.

My eye twitched. Why did everyone have to pay so much attention to me? Why couldn't I just keep my thoughts to myself and figure things out my own way? I hated the pressure.

But most of all, I hated that Kenzie was right.

"Why don't you invite her to the rafting trip Saturday?" she suggested. "It'll be a good time. She can even bring a friend if it would make her more comfortable."

"Are you saying I'm not her friend?" I hedged.

Kenzie lifted her hand and turned to leave. "Think about it."

As if I'd be able to think of anything else.

## TWENTY-SIX

## APRIL

MY HEART WAS BEATING QUICKLY as I walked back toward Diego's house. Instead of shorts, I'd opted for leggings and an oversized T-shirt so I wouldn't constantly be tugging at my clothing.

As I got closer, I could see him sitting at the table, in his usual T-shirt and shorts outfit. My mind immediately missed seeing him without his shirt on, but I quickly shut that thought down.

What had happened between Diego and me... I still couldn't comprehend.

He'd called my thighs beautiful.

Told me that he hated me.

And it seemed like he'd been seconds from kissing me.

Until his *girlfriend* arrived.

Even though Diego denied it, his little brother had clearly announced Miss Blonde Barbie as his girlfriend. And I couldn't compete. Nor should I want to. I would never be that kind of girl, just like she'd never be like me. Diego and I just didn't match up that way. Didn't fit like people expected couples to.

Not that anyone said anything about us being a couple. Heated moments on a private beach were much different than a public relationship in front of the entire school.

My mind was still spinning as I reached the patio. At the sound of my approach, Diego looked up from the snacks. "Mom outdid herself today."

So we were pretending nothing happened.

Got it.

I put my drawstring bag on the table and sat down a few chairs away from him. We clearly couldn't handle standing too close to each other. Especially because he smelled like saltwater and sandalwood and it brought me to distraction.

I got out my workbook with the notes I'd made for the assignment. "This week we're covering talk about bathing," I said.

Diego opened his own workbook. "Do they

mean like we're telling them they smell bad?"

Why was he making me laugh? "No, more like prepping them for bathing and talking them through the process."

He studied the paper a little longer, popping a grape in his mouth. "What do you think we should include?"

For the next several minutes, we made notes about our role play, and I tried not to stare at him. I'd never noticed the little scar on his chin. Or how his curls were slightly longer than when I first met him.

When we'd done all the prep we needed to, he leaned his phone against the citronella candle in the middle of the table and got up from his chair. I stiffened as he moved to the seat next to mine. I could smell the sandalwood on his skin, slightly stronger than before, and it was so consuming.

My thoughts flashed back to the way he'd looked at me, the way his brown eyes had flicked to my lips. The way his hand had felt covering mine, his fingertips grazing my thigh.

"Ready?" Diego asked.

I swallowed, hard, and nodded, reminding myself that he had a girlfriend. That whatever happened between us didn't matter because we disliked each other so much. Because my family required so much of me a relationship would never work. Especially since one or both of us would surely move for college.

We had to restart the recording twice because I kept fumbling over my words. When we finally got something good enough to turn in, I immediately began packing up my things.

"You don't want to stay and finish the snacks?" Diego asked.

Stunned he'd want me here longer, I said, "I'm not hungry." Mostly because I was so on edge around him. So jumpy. It was like my body remembered his touch and wanted to be prepared when it happened again.

Not when.

If.

*If* it happened again.

I lifted my hand in a wave and walked off the patio onto the sand, but I heard Diego say, "Wait up."

My heart jackhammered as I slowly turned to see him following me. He stopped a couple feet away—a respectable distance.

I waited, but he didn't speak. Finally, I lost the game of silent chicken. "Yeah?"

He scratched his neck. "I—uh. I was wondering, do you want to go rafting with me and some of my friends next Saturday?"

"Rafting?"

He nodded. "There's a river a little farther inland. It's more like floating than rafting. Should be a fun time. You can bring Sadie if you want."

My lips opened and closed as my mind struggled to come up with a response. "You want to spend time with me?"

He nodded again.

"What would your girlfriend think of that?" I asked, pained at the memory of her. She was so perfect for him. And not just in her looks—she probably didn't have the kind of baggage I always carried with me.

Diego seemed confused. "She's not my girlfriend."

"Your little brother said she was."

"My little brother's an idiot."

I couldn't help the small smile on my lips. "Is that so?"

"Kenz and I are just friends. In fact—she's getting ready for a date with another guy right now."

I hated how happy that fact made me. Didn't

my heart know not to get too attached?

"So will you come?" he asked, his brown eyes on me.

I folded my arms across my chest, looking at the water for a moment and then studying him. "This isn't some kind of prank, is it?"

His face screwed up. "What do you mean?"

I glared at him. "Like jocks getting the fat girls out to the country and running off with their clothes or something like that."

His jaw clenched—I'd upset him. "Why would you say something like that?"

"I may be new to Emerson, but I'm not new to high school." I gestured at myself. "Girls like me don't hang out with pretty people like you and your not-girlfriend unless there's something in it for you."

He stepped closer, the fire in his eyes that much more apparent at this distance. "Trust me. There's something in it for me." His eyes roved me, just as palpable as his touch had been.

A shiver went through my stomach, and I lifted my chin, trying not to show him just how much he affected me with a single look.

"So you'll come," he said. It wasn't a question.

I could only nod. There was no saying no. Not to Diego.

## TWENTY-SEVEN

## DIEGO

ON MONDAY MORNING, when I woke up and looked out my window, I saw April walking Heidi along the beach. Every so often, she'd bend down and scratch Heidi's ears or turn her away from a distraction. I smiled as she reached into her fanny pack and gave the dog a treat.

Why it mattered to me so much that she walked by my house again... I didn't want to admit. I watched her out the window until I couldn't see her perfect curvy form anymore and turned back to my bedroom, changing into my uniform.

I hated this thing. It felt so tight and restrictive with its buttons and scratchy fabric. But I didn't relish the thought of saying goodbye to my uniform either. It would mean being thrown into "real life."

Something that was quickly approaching, as my parents liked to remind me.

I didn't need reminders.

In fact, I had a meeting with our guidance counselor, Birdie, about that very topic this morning. And I had no idea how to tell her that going to college to study business sounded just as unappealing as a life without the beach.

Dreading the meeting, I got ready and went into school. Right over the school entrance, engraved in stone, was a Latin phrase. *Ad Meliora*. It meant toward better things, which Emerson Academy was supposed to be preparing us for. But me? I didn't know what I was supposed to move toward.

With a sigh, I continued down the hallway. I said hey to Xander and Terrell. Told Kenzie that April had agreed to come. And then walked the rest of the way to Birdie's office.

She had the door open, and I could hear her talking to her pet bird. "Ralphie boo, I know you liked the last brand, but I already told you it was discontinued. This one has all the same ingredients as the last one."

Amused, I knocked on the door. She sounded like my mom trying to convince Mateo to eat corn tortillas instead of the flour ones he preferred.

"Come in," she called.

I walked in, setting my bag in an open chair. "Ralphie doesn't like his new food?"

Birdie threw her hands in the air, exasperated. "He's so finnicky. Finch-icky?" She paused. "I feel like there's a joke in there somewhere. But I just need to find a new mix he likes."

My chuckle was strained. Birdie arguing with her bird? That was funny. But I had other things on my mind.

"You can shut the door," she said.

I did and went to sit down. Before she could ask, I said, "I still have no idea what I want to do and no plans to go to college."

She let out a breath, a small smile on her face. "You sound like your sister—except she wanted to be a rock star."

"I bet you thought *she* was the crazy one," I said. Just a year ago, Des was a talented singer with a decent YouTube following. Now? She was about to start her first concert tour as the headliner.

"She always had a spark." Birdie smiled, settling back in her chair. "Talk to me. What do you like to do?"

"I like surfing."

"And football?" she asked.

I nodded. "Don't tell Coach, but it's really just something fun to pass the time."

Her eyes twinkled as she pretended to zip her lips closed. "How are CNA classes going? Any thoughts about a medical career?"

"They're good, but I don't think I'm going to find some kind of hidden calling."

She nodded, pursing her lips in thought. "What about marine biology?"

I shook my head. "Science is not my strong suit."

Ralphie cooed from his cage, and as if she'd gotten the idea from him, she said, "Have you thought of becoming a surf instructor full-time?"

"I'm not sure I could make enough money during the off season," I said. "It would be hard to keep up with my own expenses in this area."

"Have you heard about product versus service-based businesses?" she asked.

I wracked my brain for everything I could remember from my economics class last year, which to be fair, wasn't much. "Not really."

Ralphie cooed like he was chastising me.

Birdie smiled. "We had a girl graduate here a couple years ago, Jordan Junco. Do you remember her?"

I cringed again. "Not really." This wasn't a big school, and I still couldn't remember her.

She opened her laptop and began typing on her keypad. "Jordan did keep her head down. And you would have been too young to donate blood when she was here running the blood drives..." She twisted the screen to reveal a website landing page.

## JUNCO CLEANING
Learn, do, hire, inspire.

"What is this?" I asked, scanning the text.

"A few years ago, Jordan's mother was trying to work independently as a maid. She and Jordan were barely scraping by. She'd help her mom before school, after school, on the weekends. And then her mom started a YouTube channel, started teaching courses on cleaning—both teaching people how to clean their homes and teaching others how to grow their businesses. Now she's getting television offers, opportunities to release her own line of cleaning supplies, and she's completely paid for Jordan's way through college and eventually med school."

I lifted my eyebrows. "All from cleaning?"

"And related services." Birdie nodded. "What if surfing didn't have to be 'just lessons' for you? What if it could be an entire brand?"

For the first time, I was excited about something. "Do you think that could really happen?"

"Absolutely, with the right help and training," she said emphatically. "Especially for someone like you, Diego. You understand people, and people like you. You're easy to get along with, patient, kind, and look out for others."

"I..." It was awkward, being complimented this way.

She smiled. "What you asked me to do for April? There's a reason she's friends with Sadie now, and it's big thanks to you."

The tips of my ears felt hot. "She just needed a little help."

"And so do you," Birdie said. "Jacinda has offered to mentor young entrepreneurs at the Academy. Do you want me to reach out to her and see if she could help you get started on a business plan of your own?"

"Please," I said, my voice just as hopeful as I felt.

If there was a way I could continue doing what I enjoyed and not force my life into a predeter- mined box, I would take it. I would take it in a heartbeat.

SADIE LOOKED at me over the top of a rack of swimsuits, her hair dark purple today instead of her usual turquoise. "Tell me what happened again?"

I laughed. "This is the fourth time!"

"I know," she said, "but it's so dreamy." She held a swimsuit against her chest. "Hot surfer guy pulls you from the waves, tells you he loves your thighs, and then kisses you breathless. *Swoon*."

"That's not what happened," I said, laughing again.

"So maybe I took some creative liberties." She shrugged. "Bet the kissing part will happen this weekend, though."

I cringed. "I'm still unconvinced he's not

bringing me out there for some kind of prank that'll go viral on social media later."

Sadie shook her head at me. "He's not like that."

I hoped she was right.

My eyes landed on a dark blue swim top with ruffled straps. I held it up for Sadie to see. "What do you think about this?"

Her eyes widened. "It's beautiful."

"You think?" I asked.

She nodded, coming around the clothing rack to take it in. She held it up to my chest. "The color is great with your skin tone, and it'll bring out your eyes."

I smiled, still in disbelief that I had a girlfriend to go shopping with this soon after moving to a new town. I could go a whole year at a new school without finding someone as welcoming as Sadie had been. She'd admitted to me earlier that she had social anxiety, which explained our awkward first encounters. And why she declined going on the rafting trip with me. *I don't want you to have to babysit me the whole time,* she'd said. *Have fun with Diego.*

As if I could have fun with him when just the thought of spending a day with him and his friends had my nerves on edge and my mind spiraling with thoughts and doubts.

"You should bring a wrap to wear with the suit," Sadie suggested, moving to a different rack. "That way he has something to *drive him crazy*."

My cheeks flushed for the millionth time that day. "Maybe not then. Not sure I could handle another run-in like that."

She stared at me over the next rack with a coy grin. "You could totally handle it."

"Okay, maybe I can, but maybe not the aftermath." I didn't do relationships. I'd learned early on that the second you got attached to someone, you'd have to leave. The only people I'd been able to count on were my parents and myself.

"My mom always says, 'Don't count your vases before the kiln's done baking,'" Sadie said.

I laughed. "I think the phrase is 'don't count your chickens before they hatch.'"

"Either way. Just go with the flow tomorrow. Maybe something happens; maybe it doesn't. You can trust your future self to handle the outcome either way."

I studied Sadie for a moment as she continued flipping through the hangers. That advice had been surprisingly wise. And true. None of the worrying

I'd done about my dad getting hurt during a deployment had prepared me any more for his injury. But Mom and I had figured it out—not perfectly, by any means, but we were all still standing.

"I think you're right."

"But text me every detail," she said. "I'll live vicariously through you."

I laughed. "Let's hope that's a good thing for you."

My mom was more excited for the rafting trip than I was. She even sent me to the store with her card to buy waterproof makeup I could wear. After she made breakfast for us Saturday morning, she came upstairs to my room with me and helped me do my hair and makeup.

We decided on French braids—which would look okay whether I was wet or dry, and she carefully applied eyeliner and mascara to bring out my eyes.

"You look so much like your dad when he was your age."

I raised my eyebrows. "Did he wear guyliner?"

She giggled and took out her phone. "I think I have a photo somewhere." She flipped through the thousands of photos she had saved until she reached a photo of them together at their senior prom. I tried not to remember that I came nine months after that date.

They were adorable—Mom was smaller than now, but she still had lots of curves and big full cheeks that stretched with her smile. Dad looked every bit the linebacker he'd been in school—well over six feet tall with broad shoulders and a strong jaw.

I studied him for a moment, noticing the similarities in our hair color, our face shape, and even our lips. "I have your eyes though."

She smiled. "And your heart is all your own. Even when you were little, you'd say or do things, and I'd wonder, where did this tiny human come from?"

I laughed. "Probably grabbed the wrong one at the hospital."

She put her arm around me and drew me close to kiss me on the cheek. "Are you excited?"

Biting my bottom lip, I thought it over. "I think I'm just nervous. I've never really dated before."

Mom nodded. "I'm glad you are now, though."

"You are?" I asked.

With a laugh, she shook her head. "Dating is a good thing. It's when you discover what you like in a relationship, what you don't like. You learn how to draw boundaries and get along and sometimes even forgive. That's an important skill in life."

She was right. And forgiveness was something I wasn't very good at... something I hadn't really considered doing when it came to Diego. But maybe it was time to forgive him his lousy first impression and look into the person he really was.

Mom glanced at her watch. "You should probably get outside. They should be here soon." *And we don't want a repeat of what happened last time a friend picked you up,* she didn't say.

Walking to my dresser, I picked up my drawstring bag I'd gotten at a Dollar General in western Kansas while visiting Mt. Sunflower. It wasn't a real mountain, but the tallest place in Kansas, out in the middle of nowhere. Mom and I had taken the trip while Dad was deployed... our last vacation, really. The bag was like my reminder that there were good times, and hopefully there would be more again someday.

"Good luck," Mom said with a smile.

I nodded, leading the way down the stairs and pausing at the front door, just to wave.

Then I heard Dad say, "Where are you going?"

I jerked, surprised to see him sitting on the couch in the living room. "Oh, um, some friends and I are going tubing today."

He smiled. "That sounds fun. Be good, kid."

Relief swept through me. "I will, Dad. I love you." I put all I had into those three words.

"I love you too," he said.

Feeling like I was on top of the world, I walked outside just in time to see a pickup pull up along the road. The back window rolled down as I walked toward the car, and I saw Diego, grinning just for me.

## TWENTY-NINE
## DIEGO

I GOT out of the car so I could open the door for her, but the view I had of April made me forget what I was doing. She had on this blue swimsuit that hugged her curves and a wrap around her waist that covered my favorite asset of hers. My hormones begged me to pull it off her, but I will-powered through it and said, "Looking good, April."

She smiled, biting her lip again. God, that drove me crazy. "Thanks."

I loved that she didn't argue about compliments like some girls did. She just accepted it like she knew I was right. Because I was.

I tore my eyes off her and stepped aside so she could climb into the back seat of the pickup.

As she got in, Xander said, "Hey, April," Like it was the most natural thing in the world that she was here.

"Hey," she said.

Then Kenzie turned in her seat, giving April a big smile. "Good to see you."

April seemed to falter, but said, "You too."

"Let's hit the road!" Xander said, gunning the engine and cranking the music.

April's laugh cut through the music, and the sound made me smile. She was only sitting a foot away from me, but with the music blaring and two people right in front of us, we might as well have been a million miles away from each other.

I wanted to get to know her better. To talk to her. Prove that I wasn't a complete jerk. So I got out my phone and tapped on the screen.

**Diego: You look beautiful today.**

I waited a moment for April to get the notification, and when she did, she pulled her phone out of her drawstring bag. She covered her mouth, laughing quietly.

"What?" I whispered to her.

She turned the phone toward me, and I scanned the screen, then my ears heated as I remembered how I'd saved myself into her phone.

*Sexy Surfer*

She looked back down at her phone, typing out a text, and I stared at my phone like I could will the notification to come through sooner.

April: Should I re-save your contact as Arrogant Boy?

Diego: Confident Man. ;)

April: There's a fine line between arrogance and confidence... and its name is Diego.

I laughed at that. It was so fun to talk with her when she let her guard down like this.

I was about to type back, but Xander said, "You know you two can just talk to each other, right?"

Busted.

April's cheeks warmed, and she put her phone back in her bag. I guess we were done with that. But Xander didn't lower the volume, so we rode in mostly silence. I couldn't draw my eyes away from her hands on the seat, the dark blue of her nail polish like she'd found school spirit somewhere along the way.

I was wound so tight that I practically jumped out of the pickup as soon as we reached our starting spot where the rest of our group was already waiting by a suburban. Terrell had the back hatch open and was slowly growing a pile of floats and inner tubes for us to ride down the river. There was even a cooler wrapped with pool noodles so we'd have something to eat and drink on the way.

"Y'all remember April, right?" I said.

Terrell and a few other guys from the football team, along with a few girls on the cheer squad, waved and said hello.

April waved back, seeming confident except for the tension in her shoulders. Deena told April how cute her swimsuit was while I went and grabbed the floats, moving them to the truck bed. When they were all in, April came to my shoulder and asked, "What are we doing?"

"We have to drive farther up the river," I explained. "This is technically the end point."

"Oh," she said, watching everyone climb into the pickup bed with the floats or into the cab. "How are we all supposed to fit?" she asked.

"We'll squeeze in," I replied, going to the back seat of the pickup. Everyone was piled in up front— Deena sitting on Kenzie's lap, a girl named Katie in the middle, and then a guy and two more girls in the back seat. They scooted over so I could have a seat, but April looked doubtfully at me.

"I'm not going to fit," she said, her voice almost

a whisper as she looked from the truck cab to the bed.

I reached for her hand, loving the way her soft skin felt against mine. "Sit on my lap."

Her eyes widened. "I'd crush you."

I laughed, pulling her up and settling her thighs on top of mine. Then I reached for the door, closing it.

She looked over her shoulder at me, her cheeks, neck, and even her ears growing redder by the second. "Are you sure this is okay?" she asked quietly. "Are you in pain? I was serious about the crushing."

Smirking, I leaned closer, my chin against her shoulder as I whispered, "If this is the way I go, I'll die a happy man."

She rolled her eyes at me and held on to the handle, trying to steady herself as we bounced over a dirt road. But I really didn't mind. I liked the steadiness I felt with her sitting on me, pressing me down into the seat. Liked the softness of her legs where they grazed against my bare calves.

In fact, the trip was over far too soon for my liking when Xander parked and it was time to get out.

She stepped out first, stepping aside while

everyone else piled out and smoothing the wrap she had around her legs. I went to the bed of the truck and found two tubes for us. As I approached her, I noticed her toying with the straps of her drawstring bag.

"Ready?" I asked.

She nodded slowly. "But I just realized I forgot to have my mom help me with sunscreen." She bit her lip like she knew it drove me crazy. "Do you think Kenzie would mind rubbing some on me?"

I extended my hand.

"What?" she asked.

"I can do it."

She gave me a look. "Are you sure?"

I rolled my eyes. "You act like I don't have younger siblings or live on a beach. It's no big deal." Especially because I liked the idea of touching her back far more than I cared to admit.

She finally passed me the bottle, and I squeezed some on my hand before resting the bottle on the hood of Xander's truck.

I ran my hands over her back, mapping every freckle, every divot of her skin and muscle. The lotion warmed under my touch, gliding easily over her back.

She pulled her straps to the side, baring her

shoulders, and now I was the one biting my lip. I needed to cool down.

I took deep breaths, but that was a terrible idea because I just got a strong whiff of my favorite scents—honey ginger and sunscreen. I looked away as I finished applying the sunscreen and used what was left over on my cheeks.

April stuffed the bottle back in her bag and frowned. "I'm sorry that took so long."

I followed her gaze, realizing everyone was already getting in the water. That was my bad. Maybe I took longer than I needed.

"Xander!" I yelled. "Toss some waters on shore!"

He saluted me, then reached into the cooler, throwing a couple waters back for us. They landed on the slow-flowing riverbank.

"Thanks!" I called with a smile. Secretly, I'd wanted them to take off anyway. I wanted to know more about April. Maybe if she really did have a bad personality, I'd be able to get this strange fixation out of my system. Or if she had a good personality under all her rough edges, I could finally follow this feeling that wouldn't go away.

Last week at the beach, it had been magnetic—I was unable to pull away from her once I got so close. I didn't like being out of control like that. When you spend so much time on the water, you learn your limits. When to push harder and when to back down.

But this girl was stronger than the biggest wave, and I was seconds from going under.

DIEGO NODDED TOWARD THE WATER. All of his friends had already gone around the first river bend, disappearing into a copse of trees. "Ready?"

I glanced toward the truck again, not completely sure. "We're coming back here, right?"

"Yeah, we have to."

"Great." I set my bag in the back of the truck and untied the wrap around my waist. I could feel Diego's eyes on my legs, and my cheeks felt warm again as I remembered the way his solid chest had felt pressed against my back.

He seemed so comfortable around me, but my nerves were on fire from a simple touch.

When I walked back to the riverbank, he looked like a Greek god, stepping into the water with the tubes at his hips. The gentle stream folded around his calves and continued, unperturbed by his presence.

I tested the water with my toes—cool but not too cold—and followed him in until we were waist deep. Standing this close to him reminded me of the last time we were in the water. How he'd tugged on my leash and reminded me he was there for me.

I had the same feeling now, like it was just the two of us, even though his friends were only a hundred yards or so ahead.

"I'll hold your tube while you get on," he offered.

I thanked him, sliding into the tube and resting my shoulders back against it. He sloshed onto his own and then said, "Hook your leg on mine so we can stick together?"

I lifted my leg, resting it next to his. The heat between our skin was undeniable. In contrast, my other foot dangled in the cool water, keeping the sun from being too hot.

For a moment, we just floated, the occasional laughter from ahead and the breeze the only sounds. I chanced a glance at Diego, seeing him resting his head back on the tube, completely at peace like he only ever seemed to be when he was in the water. He was confident all the time, with his swagger and easy smirk, but this was different somehow.

He peeked one eye open, and I turned my gaze down. *Embarrassing.* He totally caught me staring.

His laugh was soft and then faded away. "I'm glad you came out here with me."

The warmth from the sun spread to my chest, all thanks to his words. "Me too." I took a deep breath of the fresh air, free of the salty, fishy smell at the beach. "It's nice out here."

"Agreed." He was quiet for a moment, then, "Tell me about your last school."

I shifted in the tube so I could see him better, and he sat up as well. Light scattered over his face as we entered the trees and some of their leaves blocked the sun. He was Mowgli, Tarzan, and George, so beautiful amongst the trees.

"My last school... it was bigger than Emerson Academy."

He raised an eyebrow. "That's it? Bigger?"

"I was there longer than anywhere else, but I didn't have a lot of friends or anything. I've only heard from one of them since I've been here."

He frowned. "What do you mean, longer than anywhere else?"

"My dad usually got PCSed every three years."

"PCSed?"

"Permanent change of station," I said. "We've lived in Kansas, Colorado, North Carolina, Hawaii when I was really little. I was born in Germany."

"Wow," he breathed. "You've seen so much of the world."

I had. But I'd never found a place that felt like home. "Where have you traveled?"

"Last summer when my sister went on tour with Jude Santiago, I tagged along. Mostly to make my parents feel better about her being on her own."

My jaw dropped. "You were on the Summer of Santiago tour?"

Light danced in his eyes. "I was."

"Tell me everything. Was Jude a picky star? Did he only eat green M&Ms?"

"I won't tell. He's like family." He smiled gently, letting me know he meant it. "Before that, we'd been on a few family vacations, a couple trips to Mexico. Nothing major, like Kenzie going to Greece for an entire summer."

Why did him talking about Kenzie bother me so much? I didn't like the jealous feeling stirring in my chest. "How long have you and Kenzie been friends?"

"We've both gone to the Academy since kinder-garten. And classes are small enough that you really get to know someone if they've been around that long."

I could understand, even if I couldn't imagine. Knowing someone that long, outside of your family, seemed out of this world. "But surely there are other girls in our class you've known that long."

"Some of them." He shrugged. "I can't say too much, because it's Kenzie's story to tell, but after some guy broke her heart freshman year, we just kind of agreed to go to school dances together, and our friendship grew from there."

"You haven't wanted to date anyone?"

He met my gaze for a moment. "I didn't want to date anyone until I knew they were going to be something special to me."

All the air whooshed from my chest like the words had physically hit me.

It was a big deal that he'd asked me here.

And I wasn't sure how to feel about that.

"What about you?" he asked. "No boyfriends in Kansas?"

I bit my lip, worried to tell him the real reason I'd never had a boyfriend, trying to remind myself why I shouldn't have one now. "It's never been worth it to start something I knew would end."

"Because of the moving?" he asked.

I nodded, trying to focus on the warmth of his leg against mine instead of the sinking in my stomach.

"But now that your dad's not in the military, you can stay here longer."

I hesitated. "Theoretically."

"Are you going somewhere else to college?"

I bit my lip. "I don't know."

And you know what Diego did? He freaking laughed. "At least I'm not the only one who has no idea what I'm doing."

"I know what I want to do. It's just the location that's tricky..." I realized he didn't know the big reason I wanted to stay. My mom was my best friend, my ride or die, but she needed me too. Taking care of Dad on her own wasn't fair, even if she now had the center helping five days a week. It wasn't enough.

I bit my lip again, not sure how much I wanted to tell him. I'd barely even told Sadie anything about my dad.

Diego raised an eyebrow like he was prompting me.

I let out a breath. "My dad was injured in Afghanistan. Someone near him stepped on an IED. His shoulder and face caught the brunt of it. Between the brain injury and his PTSD, it's just best for him not to be around people who don't... understand his triggers and know how to avoid them." Mom and I were still learning his triggers, three years into recovery.

Diego let the quiet settle between us. The story was short, but the truth was heavy.

There was nothing that could repay what our family had lost. No amount of money or worldly comforts could take away Dad's injury. The deaths of other people in his platoon. It was a price, a heavy, irreversible one.

I prepared myself for Diego to change the subject like most people did when things got too heavy, but instead, he looked me in the eyes. "I think it's amazing you want to go into nursing, that you want to support your mom, after all that. Most people would run from their problems. You might be the bravest person I know."

A small sense of pride bloomed in my heart. With everything Mom and I dealt with, there wasn't much time left over for recognition, praise. "Thank you. That means a lot." More than he knew. And with each second that passed, I was realizing just how much I'd misjudged him. "You know, you're not as bad as I thought you were," I teased with a small smile.

He laughed. "I've wanted to say I'm sorry for that first day, when Heidi ran up to me on the beach."

I shook my head. It seemed silly now, compared to everything else we'd just talked about.

"Really, I should have known the second I saw Heidi," he said. "She clearly has a mind of her own."

I laughed. "Can you blame her for wanting to get close to you?"

He sent me a grin that made me melt. "The real question is why she'd want to get away from you."

## THIRTY-ONE

## DIEGO

THE MORE TIME I spent with April, the more I loved her expressions. The face she made when she was annoyed, happy. And now the cute blush she wore with a repressed smile tilting her lips.

All of her faces were beautiful.

Even the sad ones.

And I wanted all of her faces to be mine.

Her expression changed to thoughtful. "I'm surprised you don't have a grand plan for after graduation. Mom said practically everyone at the Academy goes to Ivy League schools and works high level jobs right out of college."

My frown was instant.

Just going to school at the Academy was a pressure all its own. All the teachers reminded you from the first day of school that your life was building toward graduation, toward the moment you could go into the world and change it for the better.

Admitting I just liked surfing and hanging out on the beach seemed like a failure until I had my meeting with Birdie and she encouraged me to follow my desires. She was the first person who'd done that for me.

"I'm actually meeting with a mentor next week to talk about how I can turn teaching surf lessons into a business."

April's face brightened. "You'd be good at that."

I trailed my fingers through the water and tried not to let the compliment make my chest puff up. "We'll see how the meeting goes."

"You don't sound too hopeful."

"I'm afraid of how hopeful I am," I admitted. "I don't really have a backup plan, and I don't see myself in a college classroom for hours a day. It takes about all I have to sit through these classes now."

She laughed. "You do fidget a lot."

I opened my mouth to argue, but then I grinned. "You've been watching me in class."

Her cheeks heated. "No."

"Liar." I grinned way too big. "You've been watching me."

Her eyes slid over me, and I became very aware that I was shirtless. That she could see the body I'd built from hours in the water or on the football field. My pride swelled slightly when she didn't look away.

"You're hard to miss," she finally said.

"I'll take it," I replied.

She dipped her hand in the water and splashed me. "You're so cocky."

I splashed her back. "Confident."

She dug her hand in the water, soaking me even more. "Over-confident."

"Self-assured." I splashed back.

"Arrogant." She went to splash me again, but lost her balance, tumbling out of the tube.

Laughing, I hopped off mine to grab the tube for her and tossed both of ours to the grassy banks of the slow-moving river.

She came up sputtering, pieces of hair free from her braid plastered to her face.

I laughed even harder.

Which she did *not* like.

With an evil gleam in her eyes, she tackled me under the water, and I was so caught off guard, I went down with her, far too aware of her curves pressed against my body.

When we came up, she said, "Ha!"

I wasn't laughing.

I was too busy noticing her face, inches from mine.

The dip of her swimsuit.

Her hips, barely clearing the water.

Her lips, parting in surprise.

Her eyes wide.

Her breath shallow.

Everything around us slowed, blurred, disappeared except for her.

There was no more waiting, no more holding back when it came to April Adams. I couldn't, even if I wanted to.

On instinct alone, I put my hand at the back of her neck and brought her to me. Our lips collided in the headiest kiss of my life. The soft scent of sunscreen and water on her skin, the cushion of her lips, the press of her body against mine.

It blew me away. Everything I thought it could be and somehow more.

Her hands went to my bare shoulders, heating my skin more than the sun ever could. I loved the soft feel of her fingers over my shoulder blades, her body pressed against mine. It was so easy to get lost in her, to take my time tasting her lips, deepening our kiss as the river wound around us.

But she pulled back, her lips pink, her eyes bright. "Should we get going so we're not even farther behind?"

I didn't give a crap if they had to wait on us for hours if it meant more of her kiss, but she was already pulling away, getting the tubes for us.

I took a breath, attempting to stifle the sense of whiplash falling over me.

That had been the best kiss of my life, but she was ready for it to be over far too soon.

"Here," she said, passing me the tube. She got in on her own this time, and I did the same. But she didn't offer to link us together, and instead, we floated, disconnected, down the river, quiet.

But I didn't need to tiptoe around. It didn't have to be so difficult. "What gives?" I finally asked.

She jerked her head toward me, as if surprised that I'd spoken. "What do you mean?"

I narrowed my gaze. "We kiss and then you won't even link tubes with mine."

"We can link up," she said from a few feet ahead of me, falsely cheery. "It's kind of fun to spin, though."

So now she was acting like this was *fun*? I'd never had less fun, knowing we could kiss like that and she could pull away so fast. "April."

She flushed. "I don't know what you want."

"I want to date you," I said, a little louder than I had to. Probably because I was embarrassed. I wasn't the guy who chased girls; I was the one the girls asked out. And yeah, maybe April was right about me being arrogant in that respect, but she clearly liked me back. Why did it have to be so freaking hard?

"And then what?" she demanded. "What happens when it all falls apart?"

"Why does it have to?" I asked.

I could hear our friends in the distance, gathering their things on the riverbank. But my focus was on April.

Her eyes were as dark as her wet hair as she said, "When you're a military brat like me, you learn pretty quickly that everything has an ending, and not all of them are happy."

WHEN WE GOT CLOSER to the banks, a few of Diego's friends started catcalling us, and my cheeks instantly got hot. Partially because we'd been doing what they expected of us. That kiss was...

Earth shattering.

I'd never experienced something so all-consuming. Something that had the strength to destroy my willpower and light my soul on fire at the same time.

But Diego did that.

And when he said he wanted to date me... be more to me than just a study partner or a friend?

I panicked.

How could he speak of a future with me when he didn't know anything about what that entailed?

My family was my life, and if he wanted to date me, we couldn't have the kind of fun, carefree relationship he'd have with someone like Kenzie or her friend Deena.

Life with me would be complicated for him.

We wouldn't be able to hang out at my house like other couples, and I couldn't go out too often because it wasn't fair to leave my dad at home with Mom twenty-four/seven. My best bet was to go to nursing school nearby and live at home.

Most kids our age got to imagine their futures. But ever since the injury, it was one day at a time. Dad's needs came first; mine came second. After all, Dad gave *everything* for his country, his family.

A chance at love was a small price to pay in comparison.

Diego deserved better than that.

Better than me.

It had been stupid of me to come on this rafting trip. Dumb to think my life could be anything other than what it was.

Diego and I reached the riverbank, and I stood from the float, letting the water ebb around my waist as I walked to the edge, Diego carrying my tube.

Kenzie offered me another bottle of water and

a towel, and I tried as hard as I could to smile as I took them. "Thanks."

She smiled kindly. "No problem. Did you have fun?"

I felt Diego's eyes on me as I nodded. "You?"

"Oh yeah," she grinned, holding up the water-proof phone case she wore around her neck. "This thing is amazing."

I wished I would have thought of that. My phone was back in Xander's truck, and I needed to text Sadie. Immediately.

I talked to my mom about everything, but I couldn't talk to her about this. She would tell me to follow my heart, to spend time with Diego, even though we both knew that wasn't realistic. In fact, I'd probably be making an emergency trip to Sadie's family's art studio tonight if I didn't get a good phone call in.

"Hungry?" Deena asked me, reaching into a cooler. She looked so cute in her little string bikini. Her stomach didn't even hang over when she bent over. My mom would say something like all bodies are different. All bodies are beautiful. I tried believe her.

"Um, yeah," I said.

Deena passed me a sandwich and a snack bag

of carrot sticks. I laid my towel out on the ground beside Kenzie and sat, eating lunch. I was hungry. And when I got stressed out, I ate even more.

Air brushed over my arm, and I looked over to see Diego spreading his towel beside me. Surprised he even wanted to sit by me, I cast him a curious look.

But he just smiled softly, eating his sandwich. Why was he so easygoing? I felt like I could jump out of my skin at any moment, and here he was, relaxed as ever. *Cool as a cucumber*, my dad used to say.

"Are you going to the game next Friday?" he asked me.

I raised my eyebrows, stunned he would ask. But he waited patiently for my answer.

"If Sadie wants to go," I said finally.

Diego smiled, looking at his sandwich. "I'll make sure she wants to go then."

I laughed. "Sadie's not much of a football fan."

"Even after seeing me in my football pants?" he teased with a smirk.

I shook my head at him.

Kenzie laughed. "You'll get used to him after a while."

But the truth was, I didn't know if I'd ever get

used to Diego or the way he made me feel. Like I could hope for a different life. One where butterflies were a happy feeling instead of a harbinger of things to come.

"You should come to Waldo's with us after," Kenzie said. "They make the best milkshakes."

I tried to catch any hint of nastiness in her American-girl smile, but I couldn't find it. She seemed genuinely kind. And it made me wonder even more why Diego was with rough-around-the-edges me when I was so different from her. "That sounds fun," I said at last.

One of the guys called her over to where they stood by the SUV, leaving just Diego and me quietly eating.

I could feel his eyes on me. Immediately, I became self-conscious. Of the way I chewed and how it made my double chin move. Of how my stomach looked so big, especially when sitting down. Of my hair, which was probably a tangled mess at this point.

*What did he see in me?*

I sat a little straighter and quietly said, "I'm sorry about earlier. I just don't want to hurt you."

Diego had lived in one place his entire life. He didn't know that the more attached you got to a place, to the people in it, the harder it was to leave.

And we always left.

I didn't know how to stay.

Didn't know how to even let myself dream about the things Diego had offered. Could I picture myself in a dress at homecoming, letting him spin me around the dance floor? Or what about another surf lesson, our bodies heating even in the cold water? Holding my books in the hallway? Was I that kind of girl? Could I let myself be?

But Diego looked at me for a long moment before saying, "That's always a risk you take in a relationship, which is why I haven't dated anyone before you. Believe me when I say I've thought this through, and I want to take this risk, with you."

I bit my lip, trying to deny myself what every single cell in my body wanted. But Diego was far too beautiful, too different. And me? I was far too selfish to turn him down.

## THIRTY-THREE

# DIEGO

I COULDN'T WIPE this stupid smile from my face. Not on the ride back to the truck. Not while we drove back to Emerson, taking notes for our group project. Not even when we dropped her off and Xander and Kenzie gave me so much crap for the way I looked at her.

They said I looked like a lost puppy dog.

No, I was just happy. Thinking about a girl for the first time in so freaking long. Before I met April, dating seemed like such a drag. I'd watched my sister get her heart broken almost beyond repair. Seen guys on the football team lose their minds over girls. Watched Kenzie struggle after breaking up with her first boyfriend. I wanted no part in it.

Now I knew I just hadn't found the right person

yet—the one who kept my mind spinning and my heart pounding.

Xander dropped Kenzie off at her house, and then I had to get home and prepare for my first meeting with Jacinda Junco. Jittery energy worked its way through my system, reminding me just how much was riding on this meeting.

My entire future.

I finished showering and went upstairs to get my notebook with the questions Birdie said I should ask along with a few of my own. Mom, Adelita, and Marisol worked in tandem in the kitchen, making breakfast burritos for the dance competition tomorrow in a town a couple hours away. I got out of going because I needed to work on homework with April. And I tried not to overthink the fact that we'd be alone in my house.

When Mom saw me at the island with my notebook, she looked up from the stovetop and smiled. "Ready for your meeting?"

I nodded. "Getting there."

"It's exciting, right? Learning from someone who's living their dream. A Latina no less."

"It is," I agreed. I hadn't even thought of the fact that Jacinda was Hispanic as well. Just one more sign that this could work. That I didn't have to follow the path everyone else did. This day was just getting better and better.

"Did you have fun with your friends?" Mom asked, looking up from the foil sheets she was working with.

My smile gave me away.

"Aha," she said, grinning back. "Too much fun."

"Just the right amount." I gestured at the growing stack of food. "Do you mind if I take one? I'm hungry."

Adelita huffed from the sitting room couch, where she was playing games on her tablet. "What else is new?"

I stuck my tongue out at her and said, "I knew you were my favorite, Marisol."

Marisol giggled from the opposite couch. "Back at you."

Adelita scowled. "Get out of here."

Mom shook her head at us as I grabbed a burrito and said, "Don't mind if I do."

I got in my car and drove toward Seaton Bakery, where Jacinda and I had agreed to meet. The place was unassuming—a plain boxy building painted white with a gravel parking lot that looked like it may have been asphalt at one time.

Hand lettering on the windows advertised a coffee and donut special, along with support for Seaton High School. If only the words could tell me what would come. If this meeting was just getting my hopes up or if a future outside of the norm was actually possible for me.

With a deep breath, I turned off my car and walked inside, instantly spotting Jacinda. She had lightly tanned skin and an abundance of black curls flowing down to her shoulders. Both she and the woman she was talking to at the counter turned my way.

"Diego?" Jacinda said. "Great to see you. This is Gayle—she and her husband own the place."

I smiled, in my element. I liked meeting people. "Can't wait to try out some of your food," I said, my eyes zoning in on a glass cabinet full of pastries. "It looks amazing."

Gayle beamed at me, crow's feet creasing around her blue eyes. "Pick anything you want. It's on the house."

Jacinda gave the woman a chastising look. "Gayle, you know I can pay now."

"Your money's no good here. And neither is yours, Diego. What looks good?"

I contemplated the offerings for a minute.

They had massive muffins, cupcakes, and even a row of donuts that had my mouth watering. "Can I try the Oreo cupcake and get some coffee to go with it?"

"Of course," Gayle said. "What about you, hon?" she asked Jacinda.

Jacinda ordered a bagel and a tea, and soon we were sitting in a corner booth, trying our food and making small talk about Seaton Bakery and Emerson Academy.

"My daughter had the best time at that school," Jacinda said. "I'm so happy I can give back to some of the students."

A nervous flutter struck up in my chest. "I'm really thankful. I don't know how much Birdie told you, but this is kind of a lifeline for me."

"What do you mean?" Jacinda asked.

I looked down at my cupcake, pulling the wrapper away from the sponge. "I've never really been great at school. I get along okay with mostly Cs and a few Bs here and there, but it's not really enough to get into a great college. Even if I got into one, I don't know what I'd study. All I'm really good at is playing sports, and I don't like the idea of becoming a PE teacher or coach and going back to school all over again."

Jacinda chuckled. "It sounds like you know yourself more than you think."

I raised my eyebrows. It was strange to hear after feeling so lost.

"Some of us aren't meant to go to college," she said. "And that's okay. My daughter, Jordan? I'm pretty sure she could go to school for the rest of her life and be happy as a clam. Me? I start sweating the second I get near a classroom. I like to do things, get my hands dirty, see the results of my work."

I nodded. "That's exactly it. I'm better at doing than learning from a book."

"There's lots of learning that needs to happen when you have your own business," she said. "But it's more enjoyable, for me at least, because there's a real purpose behind it. A mission. So the first thing I want us to do is write your mission statement."

The brakes of my excitement slammed and skidded to a halt.

A mission statement? This felt really similar to my economics class—the parts I could remember.

Without me even speaking, she said, "Owning a business isn't something you just set up and people will come. It's hard work, Diego. It comes with a learning curve and plenty of failure. If you don't have a good mission statement, a 'why' behind what you're doing, it'll be too easy to quit."

"I don't quit." The words were out of my mouth before I even thought them.

"So, tell me why you want to own a surf-related business?"

"Because it's all I know."

"You could always learn more," she said.

Frustration had me gritting my teeth together. "I don't want to do anything else."

"But why?" she asked.

When I couldn't answer, she stood up and pulled her purse over her shoulder. "Call me when you've figured out your mission statement."

I stood up, fear filling my chest. "We can't work on a business plan or anything else?"

"It wouldn't matter if we did."

MOM and I sat on the front porch with Sadie on speaker phone while I told them everything about the rafting trip. The only thing I left out was the sweltering heat of our kiss in the river. (What little I did tell them had my ears and cheeks on fire.)

It felt like telling them about someone else's life, despite the butterflies skirting my stomach and the heat lingering on my skin. Wasn't I supposed to know better than falling like this? Hadn't I seen every wrong way a love story could play out?

And yet, here I was, giggling with my mom and my new friend about a boy who I'd once considered an enemy.

"We have to go dress shopping," Mom said.

"He hasn't even asked me yet," I said.

"But he asked to date you," Sadie replied, "so he'll definitely ask you to the dance."

Mom nodded. "Sadie, you're going to the dance, right?"

Sadie hesitated. "Maybe? I don't want to be a third wheel."

"Either way," Mom said, "we should go dress shopping. It's always fun to try on pretty dresses and feel like a princess for a day."

I could hear the smile in Sadie's voice as she said, "That does sound like fun."

Mom and Sadie hadn't even met in person, and here they were, talking like old friends. I loved it. Even if I got that fearful feeling in the pit of my stomach, like it was all going away soon.

When we got done talking and hung up with Sadie, I got up from the porch swing, pushing the blanket aside so I could go up to bed, but Mom said, "Wait up."

I sat back down, giving her a questioning look. "What's up?"

She scratched under her nose and then said, "Your guidance counselor called me today."

My stomach sank like I was being called to the principal's office or something. "What? Why?" I shouldn't have been in trouble or anything. And my grades were good as far as I knew.

"She just wanted to make sure I understood the way they do future planning at Emerson. You're on her schedule for next week, and you'll sit with her, talk about what you're thinking of doing after high school, and I realized in the move we haven't even talked about your college applications." A wave of regret crashed over her face. "I'm feeling so awful I let it slip, April."

"It's not your college education, Mom. It's mine. It's my responsibility."

She shook her head. "You're still my daughter. I got so caught up in the move and work and taking care of your dad that I lost sight of something really important. You're only going to be here for a few more months, honey."

My chest constricted. "I have eight months until graduation, Mom. That's a lot of time to plan."

"I know it feels like you have all the time in the world, hon, but it'll go by in the blink of an eye. And with the way college applications work, you have even less time than that to make a decision."

I didn't like the way she was beating herself up, especially since I planned to go to college nearby so I could help her out. It wasn't like I was narrowing down colleges across the entire country—just the ones here.

"I'll figure it out," I promised. "And I'm sure Mrs. Bardot—Birdie—can help me with some options. Don't stress, okay?"

Her smile was gentle. "I'm your mom. It's my job to worry about you."

I shook my head, getting up to give her a kiss on the cheek. "I'm going up to bed. I'll see you in the morning."

"I love you. Goodnight."

"Love you too."

On the way in, I could hear my dad's snores coming from his room. I stood at the foot of the stairs, listening for a moment. I loved hearing the sound. It was one of the first sounds I heard from him in the hospital when they removed his breathing tube.

Sometimes, if I closed my eyes, I could imagine life was the way it used to be when I heard him sleep like this. I pictured him getting up in the morning, making breakfast for Mom and me, taking us out to a new museum or a restaurant we hadn't tried before.

He used to say that was his favorite part about being in the military. Moving so often meant he got to enjoy the world. See so many different things. And he had. The life he'd lived before his injury had been full—of experiences, fun, and love.

"I love you, Daddy," I whispered to myself and then went up the stairs to get ready for bed.

## THIRTY-FIVE

## APRIL

WHEN I WENT downstairs the next morning, Dad was in the living room, watching TV. At the sound of me coming down the stairs, he looked my way. "Good morning, monkey."

I smiled at him. "Morning, Dad."

"What are you up to?" he asked.

"Have to go walk the neighbor's dog and hope she doesn't run away again."

He chuckled, the sound warming my heart. "Hang on tight to that leash."

"I will," I promised. When I looked up, I could see through to the kitchen table where Mom was smiling at us. She gave me a thumbs-up before I turned and walked out the door.

Every bit of me wanted to stay in there with

Dad, watch TV with him and soak in these moments where he was most himself, but I knew it could change on a dime.

So I left with a smile to the Pfanstiels' and picked up Heidi and she pranced alongside me, hardly ever getting distracted or pulling on the leash. I was so proud of her... and of myself for training what I thought was an untrainable dog. After dropping her back off with Jesse, and getting another twenty-dollar bill, I walked along the shore to Diego's house. My heart beat quickly, like it hoped I'd get another kiss like the one the day before.

When I got closer to his house, I saw him outside on the patio. A beachy god in his swim trunks and an oversized Hawaiian-type shirt he wore half open. The peek at his chest muscles had my jaw dropping. I tried not to stare, but it was harder when his eyes landed on me and he sent me one of those grins that made even the sun seem dull in comparison.

I lifted my hand in a wave, hoping he liked the way I looked in this outfit. It was an orange romper with a white floral print that my mom had gotten me. I liked the way it flowed around my body and showed off my legs.

"You're looking *fine*," he said, biting his lip.

I giggled. *Giggled*. "You're not so bad yourself."

"Had to look good for my hot project partner."

Hot? Me? I'd take the compliment any day. "Keep talking like that and this blush is going to be permanently stuck on my cheeks," I replied.

"Good," he said. "I like it when your face is all red."

When he talked to me like this, it made me wonder why I'd been so hesitant, even if there was a worry in the pit of my stomach that everything would go wrong. That I'd end up with a broken heart.

"We should work on our homework, right?" I said, already knowing that focusing would be next to impossible. Especially now that I knew what kissing him felt like.

"Sure," he replied, walking back to the patio table and sitting in one of the chairs. I sat a chair away from him—I needed the space to think if we were going to get any work done. A glance at the table showed a bowl full of mango and watermelon, sprinkled with dots of red.

"What is this?" I asked

He poked a mango with a toothpick and

popped it in his mouth. "Fruit with chili and lime. Makes it taste a million times better. Try it."

A little hesitant, I reached out and used a tooth-pick to pick up a piece of mango. As soon as I put it in my mouth, the blend of savory, sour, and sweet flavors kicked all of my taste buds. It took all I had not to moan. "Have I mentioned I love your mom?"

He chuckled. "Stop making me jealous of my mom."

Why was it so easy to smile around him? I'd never been this girl, the one giggling and laughing and having fun with a guy. But... I liked it.

The back door opened, and we turned to see one of his younger sisters sobbing. She couldn't have been more than ten.

My heart instantly broke for her, and Diego moved fast, getting up from his chair and going to her. "What's wrong?"

His mom came out the door behind him. "Grandma is feeling dizzy and I need to take her to the ER, so Dad's going to take her to dance, but I can't do her hair."

I could tell Mama De was frustrated and worried, even if she tried to deliver the explanation kindly. I was about to offer to help, when Diego said, "I've got it, Mom. You go ahead."

"Thank you," she said, coming to kiss her daughter and then Diego on the forehead. "Your dad has the other two getting ready upstairs." She looked at me apologetically. "Sorry to interrupt your study session, April."

I shook my head quickly. "Family comes first." That, I understood completely.

"Exactly right," she said. Then she gave a final wave and walked around to the back garage door.

Diego's sister was still crying, and her voice broke as she said, "I really wanted the fish braid bun for today, because that's what all the other girls are wearing, but Dad can only do the twist bun and Marisol is too busy to help me."

Part of me wished I could go back to being that young, when a hairdo was my biggest worry, another part ached for her and the distress she was clearly feeling. Another part of me wished I was better at doing hair so I could help.

"Let's go to your bathroom," Diego said. "I can do the braids."

I gave him a skeptical look he didn't catch, but his sister just nodded, seeming to settle.

"I can go home," I offered, not wanting to get in the way.

"Nonsense," Diego said. "This will just take a little while. Adelita, this is April. April, Adelita."

His sister sniffed, looking somberly my way.

I bit my lip and followed them inside. I hadn't been in their house before, only on the patio, but it was completely stunning inside. A mix of colorful modern and cozy at the same time. I drank it all in, from the family photos to the cushy couches, hoping to get a glimpse into who Diego was.

If only I could see his room.

Was he messy? Neat? Did he paper his walls with posters, or did he keep things bare and minimal?

We reached a large bathroom on the main level, and Adelita sat on the counter, her feet in the sink basin, while Diego got out a box full of hair supplies. She wrapped her arms around her legs, resting her chin on her knees, while he gently brushed out her hair.

From my spot in the doorway, I rested my head against the doorframe. He was so tender with her— a side of him I'd only seen for short moments at a time.

He caught me staring in the mirror and lifted his lips slightly. "When you have three sisters and busy parents, you get practice working with hair."

"True," Adelita quipped.

Diego used a comb to part her hair in two sections and tied one back.

"What kind of dance do you do, Adelita?" I asked.

"Mostly contemporary," she said. "I'm on the competition team, so we have meets every week, on top of practices five days a week."

"You must love it to do it that much," I said.

She smiled, looking so much like her brother. "I do."

Diego stilled his sister's shoulders. "You wiggle too much when you talk. Sit still."

She gave me a guilty smile and zipped her lips, wiggling even more. Diego gave an exasperated roll of his eyes and then continued braiding. He worked quickly with her hair, feathering the strands over his fingers to form a pretty fishtail braid. It was stunning, watching this strong guy be so delicate with his little sister.

Soon the first braid was finished, and he moved on to the next one. He hummed softly as he went, a song I didn't recognize but instantly loved. His sister might have been a budding musical star, but the boy had rhythm.

When he finished the second braid, he teased

and twisted the ends until she had a bun at the base of her neck.

"Take a look," he said, giving her a handheld mirror so she could see the back.

She twisted and angled herself to get a view of her whole do. She had him add a few pins to keep it in place, and then a smile spread on her face. She jumped from the counter into his arms, holding him tightly.

"Thanks, bubba," she said, her voice muffled by his shoulders.

"Any time, baby girl."

As I watched them together, I knew falling for him was just as inevitable as our heartbreak.

## THIRTY-SIX

# DIEGO

THE NEXT MORNING, I got to school early. I wasn't sure what time April usually arrived. I only knew I needed to be there when she did.

So I parked my car and walked to the bench. Said good morning to a few of the guys from the football team walking by. Some of the cheerleaders.

Then Xander dropped his backpack on the ground and slid onto the bench next to me. "I got the worst sunburn this weekend."

I snorted, still scanning the parking lot for April. "Didn't Deena help you put sunscreen on your back?"

"She was supposed to," he huffed. "But there's a big strip of skin she missed, and it hurts like a mother trucker." He moved his back over the edge of the bench. "And it itches."

I laughed. I shouldn't have laughed. But I did.

"You're the worst," he said.

"Maybe," I agreed.

He nodded toward the stairs. "You going in?"

My cheeks felt warm. "I'll see you in class."

He raised an eyebrow. He knew me too well.

"Okay, I'm waiting for April. Happy?"

His steely grin told me he was. "So I'm guessing Sunday went well?"

"Yes." Except we didn't get a repeat of that mind-blowing kiss from Saturday. It might have been an addiction, the way I kept thinking about her lips on mine.

"Man, you're in trouble," Xander said, getting up from the bench and slinging his backpack over his shoulders. "More trouble than a day of detention for the skateboarding fail."

He was right. Although I'd never tell him.

Not long after he left, I saw her. Her face looked focused through her windshield as she drove into the parking lot, and I lost sight of her for a moment as she parked. I got up from the bench, walking to the curb to meet her. Then I extended my hand.

Looking confused, she gave me a high five.

I laughed. "Your backpack, April."

"My backpack?"

"I'm dating you. That means I carry your books."

Her lips lifted into a shy, almost disbelieving smile. "I thought that only happened in the movies."

"You are a star," I half-joked, my hand still extended.

She slipped her backpack off her shoulders and rested a strap in my hand.

"Dang, girl, this is heavy. Are you sure you didn't add rocks or something?"

"Some of us have to study to keep our grades up," she replied, adjusting the lapel of her uniform blazer.

She had a point. If I spent more time studying, I probably could have gotten better grades, but then I would have missed out on the fun parts of life—surfing, hanging out with friends, playing football on Friday nights.

*Abuelo* always said, "Life is to enjoy." I agreed with him wholeheartedly.

"How was your night?" I asked her as we reached the stairs. I took them at her pace, not in any hurry.

"Sadie and I went to get milkshakes." Her cheeks turned slightly red, making me curious.

"You wanted to talk about me, didn't you?" I teased.

"No!" she said way too quickly.

"Uh huh, that was convincing."

"Now I'm remembering why I hated you," she replied drily.

My laugh came naturally. "I don't know why I didn't like you. You're adorable when you're mad."

Her cheeks turned redder, making me smile even more. She really was cute.

We reached the top of the stairs, and she said, "I can take my bag back if you want."

"Why?" I asked. This thing really was heavy.

She glanced down at the ground, giving me a view of the twisted bun atop her head. "I didn't know if you'd want to be... associated with me."

Okay, now I really was confused. "Why would you say that?"

She bit her lip, looking up at me now with wide brown eyes. "Are you going to make me say it out loud?"

I had an idea of where she was going, and I didn't like it one bit. I thought we'd squashed this doubt back on the beach. "Why should I be embarrassed to be with you?"

She paused as someone walked by us, then whispered, "Because I'm not your type!"

My head jerked back. "Really? Because I thought I was the one who decided that."

"I mean the kind of girl people expect you to be with. Like Kenzie. I mean, it's one thing hanging out with friends, but the whole school? I want you to be sure."

I hated that she compared herself to Kenzie. Hated that she couldn't see how hot her curves were and how captivating her personality was. But most of all, I hated that for whatever screwed up reason our society had led her to believe she wasn't worthy of a relationship with whoever she pleased.

So I wanted to make myself very clear. I stepped closer to her, leaving barely an inch between our bodies, and angled my face down to look her in those ocean-blue eyes. "You, April Adams, are exactly my type," I said, my voice husky with the desire to kiss every doubt, every argument away from those beautiful lips. "Now let me carry your bag inside."

I half expected her to argue; instead, she slipped her fingers through mine.

We walked through the door into the building, and for the first time, I felt like the *Ad Meliora* inscription was correct. This was the better thing I had been waiting for.

Eyes turned toward us in the hallway. A few people waved at me, and I lifted my chin in recognition. I wanted April to see me be proud of her—she was good enough, she belonged exactly where she was, her hand clasped to mine.

We got close to first hour, and Kenzie walked up to us, thumbs hooked on her backpack straps. "Look at you two, all cute together. Deena, aren't they so cute?"

Deena walked up behind Kenzie, giving us an appraising smile. "V cute."

April laughed quietly, and I said, "She's more than cute."

Someone cleared their throat behind us, and I turned to see our English teacher standing with her arms crossed. "I'd love to hear how lovely April is, but class is about to start."

April's cheeks flamed, but I smirked. "Maybe I could get some extra credit for my sonnet writing abilities, Mrs. Morgan?"

She laughed and said, "Get in class, Fabio."

I had no idea what that meant, but I gave April

a last squeeze of her hand before letting go and returning her backpack. "Until later, mi amor."

She shook her head at me, smiling all the while. She had a beautiful smile, and the only thing better? Knowing I was the one who put it there.

I REACHED INTO MY LOCKER, finding a folded piece of notebook paper. Glancing around to see if I could tell who left it, I opened it and scanned the writing inside.

*I think you look pretty good on my arm.*

I snort-laughed. Diego may not have been the kind of guy to write a poem, but he was the kind to make me laugh. To make me feel like a senior in high school instead of an adult with the weight of a family on my shoulders.

I couldn't explain to him how much that meant. But I hoped to give him back even a tenth of what he'd given me.

I put the folded sheet of paper in my backpack and then shut my locker. I was stalling, really. I had a meeting with Birdie during my current events class, and I wasn't ready. My chest already felt heavy as I walked through the thinning stream of students toward her office.

The bell rang, and the sound of footsteps on tile floors disappeared.

It was just me and this door.

I traced the name plate with my gaze.

Room 109
Birdie Bardot
Guidance Counselor

The room needed a warning sign instead.

May make you face your fears.

I took a deep breath. I'd faced harder things than talking about colleges. This would be a walk in the park.

I hoped.

I knocked on the door, and Birdie sang, "Come in."

A step into the room took me back to my first day at Emerson Academy. I'd only been here a couple months, but it felt like a million years. I already had a friend, a boy who carried my backpack for me. One who made me smile.

But this meeting was just another reminder that my next move was coming—sooner than I could even imagine.

Birdie stood behind her desk and picked up a ceramic mug. "I'm out of coffee. Mind walking with me?"

I lifted my eyebrows, surprised, and half expected her to be talking to someone behind me. Her bird cooed like I should answer, so I nodded. "Sure."

"You can drop your bag in the chair," she offered.

I did and then stepped into the empty hallway with her. Her bright pink heels tapped loudly against the tile compared to the soft sole of my leather saddle shoes. She took a deep breath and said, "I always like the hallways when they're empty like this. Lots of room to think."

I'd never really seen it like that, but she was right. The quiet was nice.

We walked past Diego's locker, and my eyes landed on the blue metal. There were cute little signs put up by the booster club. A feather quill-shaped cut out with text that said *Write in a victory!* A photo of him in his uniform in a football-shaped frame. Another one in the shape of a football helmet, his jersey number, 13, stenciled on the side.

Birdie stopped in front of a brown door.

## Room 117
### Teacher's Lounge

I was trying to decide if that apostrophe was grammatically correct when she pushed the door open, revealing an empty room with short blue carpet and a pair of worn leather couches. It smelled a little... stale.

"Have a seat," Birdie said as she walked to the coffee pot. While she filled her mug, liquid tinkling against the ceramic, I settled into the love seat, sinking into the cushion.

"Coffee?" Birdie asked.

I shook my head, already on edge without the extra caffeine.

She stirred in a packet of sugar and went to sit on the other couch. "So your mom tells me you want to be a nurse?"

I nodded.

"What path are you looking at? Do you want to start with a BSN and move into advanced nursing?"

"I haven't really thought of much beyond going to college, to be honest," I admitted.

Birdie took a sip of coffee, her bright pink lipstick leaving a mark on the mug. "I called an alumna who is working as a nurse practitioner at Johns Hopkins and talked with her about some of the different pathways. She said she's worked with people who came from all kinds of educational backgrounds, but most hospitals are looking for that BSN nowadays."

Back in Kansas, a lot of the rural areas would take what they could get. An area this populous could probably afford to be pickier, and if this is where Mom and Dad were settling, then that's what I'd do. "I'll go with the BSN," I said.

Her blond curls bounced with her nod. "Where are you thinking about, university wise? Duke is ranked highly, as are Johns Hopkins and NYU. Your mom said you've been all over the country—maybe there's a place you've been that you'd like to go back to?"

"Just here," I said. Maybe too quickly, because Birdie's lips pursed slightly.

She held her mug in both her hands, looking at the dark liquid. "Is there a reason you want to stay local?"

I bit my lip, wondering how much she already knew. If it would be worth it to avoid the truth. If she could keep this confidential from my mom. Finally, I said, "It doesn't feel right to go anywhere else."

She studied me for a long moment, then said, "The good news is there are several great schools here locally and even more within a few hours' drive. I'll gather some data and send you the application links. When you apply, just forward me the confirmation."

That seemed like an odd request. "Do colleges require your sign-off?"

"Not the colleges." She took another sip of coffee. "The way it works here at the Academy is I have to see you making significant progress toward your future plan for me to sign off on your counseling requirement for graduation."

"This school is different," I said. "In so many ways."

A slight smirk formed on her lips. "Different is a beautiful thing."

## THIRTY-EIGHT

## DIEGO

TODAY IN OUR CNA CLASS, I put my things on the table beside April's and said, "Mind if I sit here?"

She looked up at me, a coy smile on her face. "I don't know. Are you going to write me a sonnet for extra credit?"

"Ouch," I said, laughing. "Okay. Game respect game."

She laughed. "Sit down before someone realizes you took their seat."

She made a good point. Even though we didn't have assigned seating in this class, everyone had sat in the same place since day one. It was like we were all creatures of habit, finding comfort in the ordinary.

But my girl was anything but ordinary. And I wasn't giving up extra time with her because of some unspoken social rule.

So, when the college girl who usually sat next to her came into the room and saw me, she paused for a moment, like her brain was coming off autopilot. Then she took my old place toward the back. A new order established.

It only took me about five minutes to realize what a terrible freaking idea that had been.

Between the smell of April's perfume and the way she played with her hair as she took notes, I was a goner.

I could only remember a third of the words Janice said, and I had to stare at my textbook, hard, to understand those words.

It was the most torturous three hours, sitting next to her and not being able to hold her hand, to cross my ankle over hers.

On the other hand, April took notes. Studiously. She used bullet points and different colors and even drew diagrams that weren't on the board to help organize the content. She was smart. Way too smart to be sitting with a guy who couldn't smell honey ginger and remember the name of a chair lift at the same time.

It was a relief when Janice shut down the projector and said class was over. I nearly knocked my chair over getting out of my seat, making April laugh.

"Nervous for the game?"

Crap.

I hadn't been.

Until now.

Now that I remembered April would be in the stands. Not as my enemy, but as my girl.

"You're going to be cheering for our team this time, right?" I checked.

She swatted my shoulder. "Who said I was cheering for the other team?"

I raised my eyebrows.

"Okay, maybe I cheered when you got knocked down." She held her fingers up, pinching her thumb and pointer finger. "Just a little."

"Yeah, yeah," I said, grabbing up her little bag that she carried everywhere except school, where we were required to have plain-colored bags.

This one was blue and had a sunflower on it with curly text that said *ad astra per aspera*.

"What does it mean?" I asked, holding up her bag. I'd taken Latin as a graduation requirement, but all I remembered was *ad meliora* and *dulce periculum*.

She glanced at the bag, her eyes glassing over. "To the stars through difficulty. It's Kansas's state motto."

"I like it," I said, walking toward the door. "It's kind of like *ad meliora*, but with Buzz Lightyear vibes."

She giggled. "I'll be sure to let Kansas know you approve."

"You should do it fast. They've probably been holding their breath waiting for me to say something."

She looped her hands through my elbow. "So cocky."

"You like it," I teased.

"You like it enough for both of us," she said, giggling.

"Maybe." We walked through the hallway and outside the building. "So, what's on the agenda for tonight?" I asked.

"Besides cheering on my 'Sexy Surfer' boyfriend at his football game?" Her cheeks instantly flushed. "I mean. I—I'm sorry, I didn't mean to use the b-word, I..."

I set our bags on the sidewalk and held my hand to her mouth, stopping her stream of nervous words. Her eyes anxiously searched my face, but I only smiled.

"Are you done?"

She nodded.

I slowly lifted my hand away, and when she opened her mouth to speak, I covered it again, stepping closer.

"Let me go first."

She nodded, but I kept my hand in place, loving the feel of her lips on my palm.

"We don't have to play those games," I said. "I'm crazy about you, April. I'd love to be your boyfriend. As long as you'll let me call you my girlfriend."

I felt her lips twitch under my hand, and I moved it away.

She lifted her arms, linking her fingers behind my neck. "Of course I'm yours. I've been annoyed with you or infatuated with you from the moment I first met you."

"Same here, but mostly just in awe." Her eyes flicked to my lips, and I took the invitation, lowering my mouth to hers. She tasted sweet, like she usually did. But the way her body molded to mine, the way she fit in my arms, it was everything. *Everything*.

"Get a room," someone from our class called, and I broke apart from April long enough to say, "Ignore him."

## THIRTY-NINE

# APRIL

SADIE'S CAR pulled up to the house at exactly six o'clock. She didn't honk this time, but Dad still saw her out the window.

"Who is that?" he asked skeptically.

Mom and I exchanged a glance behind his back. He sounded irritated.

"My friend Sadie," I answered cautiously. "We're going to watch the football game."

Dad lifted his hand and waved. "Have fun, monkey," he said. "Your mom and I will enjoy some kid-free time."

Mom let out a startled laugh. "I guess we will."

Something felt off, even though the exchange seemed positive. I just couldn't put my finger on what it was.

"We should rent a movie," Dad said. "One of those romances you like so much."

"That sounds great, honey," Mom replied, her eyes glassy.

Maybe it was the way Mom responded, like this was both healing and breaking her heart.

I tugged at the edge of my Emerson Drafters T-shirt. It pulled tight around my broad hips. "I don't want to keep Sadie waiting."

"Go ahead," Dad said.

Risking a change in his mood, I went to Dad and hugged him tight. "Love you, Dad."

He put his arms back around me, and I let myself savor the feeling, let myself pretend everything was the way it used to be. He still smelled like he always did, like his spice cologne and the soap Mom used to wash his clothes. "I love you, April girl," he said.

When I pulled back, I noticed Mom sniff. "Here," she said, "why don't you wear my bracelet? I saw you eyeballing it earlier."

My lips parted. "Mom, are you sure?" It was her gorgeous diamond tennis bracelet—Dad bought it for her when I was born.

"I'm sure." She gave it to me, and I slipped it around my wrist, clasping it shut.

I held out my arm, gazing at the sparkling stones. "I love it, Mom."

"It's beautiful on you." She smiled. "Tell Sadie we said hello."

We.

"You know," Dad said. "Why don't we go out and say hello?" He walked toward the door, and my heart dropped.

What if this didn't go well? What if she said something that triggered his PTSD?

But he was already walking out the door, and Mom and I couldn't stop a giant of a man like him. We hurried behind him as he walked up to Sadie's car. He knocked on the window and waved with a smile on his face.

To her credit, she didn't speed away.

No, she got out of the car and gave him that kind but uncomfortable smile of hers, saying, "I'm Sadie."

Dad stuck out his hand for her to shake. "I'm Doug. April's dad. Had to meet her new best friend."

Sadie looked at me over my mom's shoulder, like she was checking for permission.

I nodded and gave her an encouraging smile.

When she looked back at my dad, she said, "April's been a great friend to me, too."

"Glad to hear that," Dad said. He stepped back and put his arm around Mom's shoulders. "Have fun, girls."

"We will," Sadie said at the same time as I said, "Thanks, Dad."

We got into her car as my parents walked back to the house. My heart was tight in my chest, always feeling like I was being pulled in two or three directions and waiting for the other shoe to drop. But I tried to hang on to the happy feeling. The one that reminded me I just got a real hug from my dad. He met my friend without anything disastrous happening. And even though his brain injury shortened his fuse and affected his memory, he wasn't completely lost, no matter how much it felt that way sometimes.

Sadie smiled over at me in the car. "You look pretty. Is that a new bracelet?"

I held up my wrist. "It's my mom's."

"Beautiful." She looked over her shoulder, pulling out of our driveway. "So that's your dad?"

I nodded, feeling more vulnerable than ever before.

"And his scars..."

"He was injured in the military," I said, finding it harder to tell her than Diego. Maybe because this friendship mattered so much to me. "Someone in his troop stepped on an IED. Dad survived, barely. A lot of his injuries are to his brain."

She nodded. "He seems nice. Your mom too."

"He is, when he's himself," I said, needing her to understand why she couldn't come over. The dad she saw, that wasn't the full picture. "He..." I trailed off, looking for the right words.

She tapped on the brakes at a stop sign and looked over at me. "You don't need to explain, April."

"You're my best friend," I said softly. "I want to tell you."

She smiled at me and nodded. "I'm here."

Relief and gratitude washed over me in equal measure. "Thanks, Say."

"No problem." She continued driving toward the school.

I filled her in on his injury, what the last three years had been like, watching him heal, watching him struggle through therapies, having strangers come to our house every day to take him to the day program. And eventually the brochure that still rested in my backpack, heavier than any book inside.

Sadie wiped a tear from the corner of her eye. "You're so strong, April."

The crazy thing was, I felt weaker than ever, letting these people in. Depending on them. But I thanked her anyway. Because this friendship thing? This vulnerability thing? It was scary, but she made me feel like it was worth it.

We were quiet for a moment, and then she said, "So how are we feeling about the game tonight? Do we still like Diego or are we back to hating him again?"

I bit my lip, holding back a thousand-watt smile. "We like him. Especially considering I'm his girl-friend now."

She screamed. "What!"

I nodded excitedly. "We made it official after class today."

"Oh my gosh, you have to tell me everything he said."

She continued driving while I went over all the details. Even how he kissed me after our classmate saw us. Like he really wanted people to see us together—he wasn't embarrassed of me in the slightest, and it was making me feel so good about myself. I knew my worth couldn't come from a guy, but he was just reaffirming all the things Mom had told me throughout my life. Proving them to be true.

"We should have brought a Diego sign like his family has," she said. "We at least need to make one by homecoming." She tapped a few buttons on her dash, and soon her mom was agreeing to have us come over and make one the following week.

"What about you?" I asked. "Anyone you're hoping will ask you to homecoming?"

She snorted, pulling into the football stadium parking lot. "I eat lunch in a locker room. Even if there was a guy who I wanted to ask me out, he wouldn't know I existed."

It wasn't exactly an answer, but she was already getting out of her car, conversation over.

I pushed open my door, stepping into the chilled night air. Even though it warmed up during the day, the cool air coming off the ocean made the temperatures drop at night.

Music drifted over the parking lot—the pep band was playing a song I recognized but didn't know the name of. Then the scent of popcorn hit my nose, making my mouth water. "Snacks?" I asked.

Sadie nodded, looping her arm through mine. "Didn't I tell you? I'm just here for the food."

I laughed. "That's my girl."

## FORTY

## DIEGO

XANDER SLAPPED my shoulder and pointed toward the stands. "There's your girl."

I followed his finger, instantly spotting April. Her brown waves spilled from a white beanie, and she wore a blue shirt with a black jacket and leggings.

I could write a love song for those leggings and the way they hugged my favorite part of her.

We locked eyes, even from this far away, and she raised her hand in a wave. I pretended to kiss my hand and throw it to her like a football. She shook her head, and I could only imagine the blush she was wearing.

I kissed my hand and threw it again. This time Sadie shoved her. April's smile was so much brighter than any of the stadium lights. She caught my kiss, holding it to her heart.

We were the kind of couple I usually made fun of, but I didn't give a crap. It felt good to know I was the one she was looking at, the one she'd cheer for during the game. That she'd be at Waldo's Diner with me tonight and my date to the home-coming dance next week.

"Diego," Coach barked. "Quit playing kissy face and warm up."

"Yessir," I said, not even a little embarrassed. I went back to the line where we were running passing drills and jumped in, reenergized. Each catch came that much more smoothly, each tackle was full of that much more fire, because my girl was watching, and I was going to make her proud.

The team finished warming up, and when the game started, I gave it my all from the first second to the last. I glanced toward the stands every so often, and when I did, April was there. For me.

I finally understood why the guys on the team would lose their minds in a relationship. Because I'd given mine away to April, along with my heart, and we'd barely started dating. We didn't have a history, like some of my friends did with their girlfriends, but we would have a history soon. We'd make one.

In the locker room after an epic win, Coach pulled me aside. "Diego, whatever you did tonight, keep doing it. Got it?"

"Yessir," I replied with a grin.

The guys and I showered up, then I got in Xander's truck with Terrell, Kenzie, and Deena to hit Waldo's Diner. I wasn't the kind of guy who cared too much about clothes, but tonight, I'd taken time to find a pair of jeans I liked and paired it with a cream-colored Henley shirt. My sister Des always called Henleys the guy version of leggings. I wasn't quite sure what she meant, but I assumed it was good.

I hoped April liked my clothes and cologne as much as I liked her looks. But to be fair, she could roll up to the diner in sweats and I'd still be drooling over her smile, her wits, the no-nonsense way she viewed the world.

From the back seat of the truck, Deena said, "Is lover girl coming to the diner?"

Xander answered before I could. "She better. Diego is way less of a pain since she came around."

Kenzie nodded. "True."

"What does that mean?" I asked, trying not to be defensive.

They all exchanged a look, and Terrell said.

"I've got this." He put his hand on my shoulder. "You were getting a little tense at the end of the summer." He placed his other hand over his chest. "I get it. Last year of school starting up had me stressed too. But it was like ever since she started at the Academy, you got your spark back."

Xander nodded. "Or maybe that dog she watches fetched that stick out your butt."

While Terrell laughed, Deena scrunched up her nose. "Gross."

"It's a good thing," Kenzie said, reassuring me. "You're happier now."

I nodded, trying not to take it personal. I didn't want my friends to see me as a pain, but I did feel better now. Not just because of April, but also because Jacinda was helping me find a direction for my life outside of the expected. Even if I was still having trouble nailing down my mission statement.

We rolled up to Waldo's Diner, and the parking lot was mostly full. I got out of the truck, looking through the diner windows to see April and Sadie sitting in a booth toward the back of the diner.

It was just the two of them, and April had her arms waving through the air, excitedly telling Sadie a story. I wished I could hear what it was about— that I could see that side of April more often.

Terrell clapped my shoulder. "Come on, lover boy. Let's get inside."

I chuckled in response, following them in. The entire restaurant cheered as we walked through the door.

The guys and Deena got pulled into a table with the cheerleaders, and Kenzie and I went to sit with Sadie and April. Sadie seemed to tense with Kenzie next to her, but she still smiled and said, "Good game, Diego!"

"Thanks," I said.

April cringed at me and said, "Am I ever going to get used to seeing you be tackled? It wasn't nearly as fun to watch now that I like you."

Kenzie laughed so hard she snorted. "I like her."

I shook my head. "You can go back to hating me for a little while, as long as you come to the games. I think you're my lucky charm."

"Yeah?" April asked.

I nodded. "Coach said I played better than I ever have tonight."

"Gah," Sadie said. "Why are you two so cute?"

"Right?" Kenzie agreed.

I smiled across the table at April, and she

returned the smile before shyly looking down. Adorable. As usual.

A waitress came by and took our orders for milkshakes, then Kenzie asked, "Did you two do anything before the game?"

Sadie and April shrugged at each other, and Sadie answered. "I just picked April up at her house, met her parents for a little bit. That was fun."

My eyes slammed to April's. Sadie met her parents? Including her dad? At her house?

April had been so nervous to even let us pick her up before the rafting trip. A strange sense of... hurt? Betrayal? Confusion? Jealousy? Bloomed in the pit of my stomach. I knew April and Sadie were friends, but I wanted April to let me in too. And this was a signal that she was still holding me at arm's length.

I extended my leg underneath the table, gently touching my calf to hers. She smiled across the booth at me.

And though I was glad she could share her smiles, I wanted more. I hoped she would let me behind her walls.

## FORTY-ONE

## APRIL

SADIE SAID the best place in town to shop for dresses was this store at Emerson Shoppes called Vestito. So, after school on Wednesday, we hit the store, hoping they would have something that fit us. Otherwise, we'd have to go to LA and hope we could find something in a specialty store that carried plus sizes.

We had about an hour to shop before the center would bring Dad home, so we were on a mission. As we walked up to the store with its curly-lettered sign, I saw Sadie and Harini out front. Instead of the paint-splattered overalls Harini usually wore, she had on tan linen pants and a floral button-down T-shirt. But her Birkenstocks carried her trademark paint stains. And instead of her school uniform, Sadie had changed into jeans and a T-shirt like me.

When we reached them, I said, "Mom, this is Sadie and her mom, Harini."

Harini reached out, taking Mom in a hug. The way they instantly hit it off, chattering about the store and the dance, I could have sworn they were long-lost best friends.

Sadie and I walked in behind our mothers, and I muttered, "Are you ready for this?"

She shook her head. "I would go to the dance in this if I could."

I laughed, mostly because I agreed. Shopping in a bigger body was a special form of torture. Even if something looked good on the rack, there was no guarantee it would actually be flattering on my body. Not to mention that sizes were never consistent across brands. I could be a twenty in one store and a twenty-eight in another. And squeezing something on over my curves or not being able to pull up a pair of pants over my thighs made me feel horrible every time.

Luckily, my mom had a great eye for these things. She usually bought my cuter clothes online and returned the ones that didn't work, but we didn't have time for that now.

Mom led the way into the store, showing racks upon racks of dresses in all colors, styles, and materials.

"I actually like having a uniform so I don't have to worry about shopping," I admitted to Sadie.

"Let's celebrate this being over with milkshakes?" she suggested.

"I'm game."

A saleswoman in a knee-length black dress approached us and smiled warmly. "Can I help you ladies?"

Mom adjusted her purse over her shoulder. "We're looking for homecoming dresses for our daughters. Can you show us the plus-size section?"

I half expected the woman to take us to a different part of the store, hidden away from all the straight-size shoppers, but she brought us to a long row of dresses right near the front.

Harini reached out to touch a shiny blue fabric. "This selection is amazing."

"We try our best to make sure all of the girls and women around here have what they need." The woman clasped her hands in front of her. "Would you like some help picking out a few styles for the girls, or are you just browsing today?"

I spoke up. "We'll look on our own."

"Great," she said. "I'll set up some dressing rooms for you two and bring the mamacitas some champagne."

Mom raised her eyebrows at Harini. "Are we in heaven?"

Harini laughed. "Pretty close."

I smiled at the two women. This was a side of my mom I hadn't seen in so long, her making friends and joking with someone other than me in stolen moments of the day.

Sadie walked toward the end of the row, flipping through the gowns, and I started a little farther down. Sadie said she wanted something simple, probably black, and I pulled out a midi-length dress with sheer sleeves. "Sadie!"

She stared at it, a small smile on her lips. "I never thought I'd like a dress."

I laughed, pulling it down from the rack. "We'll add this to the pile then."

Sadie held it in her arms as we continued searching, grabbing different dresses to try on. When our arms were so full we couldn't carry any more, we went to the dressing rooms.

As usual, there were a few options that I didn't even like enough to take out of the dressing room and show the others. But when I finally found one that fit, I grinned in the mirror.

I stepped out of the dressing room at the same time Sadie did, and my jaw fell to the floor.

It was *the* dress. The black one that contrasted her light skin and colorful hair and made her look like a total babe. "Sadie!"

"I know!" she said sheepishly.

"You look so good," I said, gently touching the sequined fabric that flared from her waist.

"I'm going to live in it," she replied, holding the skirts to her chest.

From outside of the dressing area, Mom called, "Are you going to show us?"

I gripped Sadie's hand, and we walked out of the dressing room. As soon as they saw us, Mom put her hand to her heart, and Harini covered her mouth.

"Beautiful," Mom breathed.

"Do a spin," Harini instructed.

Sadie looked at her mother like asking her to do a spin was the equivalent of asking her to prance around naked.

"Come on," I said, spinning in my dress so the skirt flared around me. "It's *fun*."

Sadie joined me, looking so uncomfortable I had to laugh.

Our moms laughed too, and my mom said, "That has to be the one, Sadie. It's gorgeous on you."

Sadie pressed her hands over her mouth, her shoulders shaking as tears began to fall down her cheeks.

Harini set her champagne glass down and went to Sadie while Mom and I exchanged a glance.

"Sadie, honey, what's wrong?" Harini asked, her thin arms around her daughter.

Sadie looked up, wiping at her eyes. "I've just never felt *pretty* before. Not like this."

Harini's eyes were moist now too. "Sadie..."

I reached out for my friend's hand, holding it as her mother held her. "Sadie, you're the most beautiful person I know. Inside and out," I said.

Smiling through her tears, Sadie said, "I'm so glad I met you."

"Me too," I replied earnestly. No one had ever made me feel so comfortable and accepted like Sadie had. She had a gift that way.

"I didn't mean to take up all the attention," Sadie said, composing herself. "Is that the dress for you?"

I'd almost forgotten the pink satin dress I had on. Looking down at myself, I said, "I think I need to try on a couple more."

We both went back to the dressing room, and while Sadie changed back into her clothes, I tried on the next couple of dresses.

When I found the one, I sat in the dressing room and stared at myself in the mirror. I imagined Diego next to me in a suit, his dark eyes glittering as he looked at me with nothing but admiration.

How was this me?

How was this my life?

And yet again, I had to thank Diego. The boy who'd taken me through waves scarier than the ocean, tugged on my leash, and let me know he was there, and it was all going to be okay.

## FORTY-TWO

# DIEGO

APRIL TOLD me she was wearing a mauve dress. I didn't know what that meant, but the woman at the flower shop did. She made a corsage with several different colors and grayish-purple ribbons. I carried the plastic box out to my car and drove back to the house to get ready for the dance.

I knew April and Sadie were getting ready together, but guys didn't really do that. I'd see Xander and Terrell when we got to the dance. I pulled up to the house, expecting to go to my bedroom and get ready until Mom forced me to take some pictures.

Instead, I saw a cherry-red car in the driveway that hadn't been there in weeks. Grinning, I got out of my car and jogged up the front steps, taking two at a time. When I walked through the front door, I spotted Des sitting at the kitchen island across from my mom.

"What are you doing here?" I asked, jogging to her and wrapping her in a hug.

She squeezed me back, laughing. "That's quite the welcome."

"I missed you," I admitted. "Figured you were too busy being famous to remember us."

She punched my arm. "Couldn't forget you even if I wanted to. Especially with Mom calling to tell me you have a *girlfriend* now and you never bothered to tell me!"

"Crap." Why hadn't I called her?

Mom answered for me, saying, "He's been all heart-eyed ever since she moved to town."

I raised my eyebrows at Mom. "How much do you know about her?" I couldn't remember saying too much.

Mom smiled. "Us moms in the neighborhood, we talk. Mrs. Gartel said she saw you giving April a surf lesson and that you two seemed *very* cozy. Then April's mom called me to make sure your outfits would match." Her eyes lit with humor. "Wonder why she wouldn't expect a teenage boy to know what color mauve is."

My ears and cheeks and neck grew hot. Sometimes I got so caught up in what I was doing I forgot about the world around me. "Did you tell Mrs. Gartel to mind her business?"

"Diego," Mom admonished, smiling all the while.

Des pouted. "Why do I know less than Mrs. Gartel? Tell me everything, Di."

"I have to get ready for the dance. Come downstairs with me and we'll talk."

Mom waved us goodbye, and my big sister and I went downstairs. All our younger siblings were playing a musical video game, Marisol standing at the front of the room, a microphone in her hands as she absolutely butchered a pop song. We walked into my room, closing the door to the music. "She did not get her talent from you," I said with a laugh.

Giggling, Des said, "There are some things I don't miss."

"Uh huh," I said, knowing she missed our family dearly. She called our mom almost every day from her new apartment near the recording studio.

I went to my closet, pulling out the dress shirt and pants I planned to wear for the dance, along with a blazer, a black belt, and tie.

"Nice fit," Des said approvingly.

"You think?" I just hoped April would like it.

"Black on black? It's classic," she said. "Now tell me about this girl that has you nervous for the first time in your life."

My ears got hot, remembering that call I made to her. No one could ever accuse my sister of being subtle. And she'd never pass up a chance to say *I told you so.* "Her name is April."

"April." She said her name like she was trying it out. "I like that. But I already knew her name. Along with everything else on her social media profile. Tell me something I don't know."

"Creepy much?" I teased, pulling off my T-shirt and changing into a black undershirt. But to be fair, I'd done the same thing. I didn't care to admit how many times I'd lain in my bed at night, just scrolling through her profile pictures.

Des asked, "What about her hobbies? What does she like to do?"

"She's flexible," I said. At my sister's raising eyebrows, I hurriedly added, "She's the kind of girl that goes with the flow."

Des nodded. "What kinds of things do you do together?"

"Mostly study," I admitted. "But we went on a rafting trip with some of my friends... I gave her a surf lesson, but everyone already knows that. We hang out at Waldo's, text sometimes in the evenings. And then the dance tonight."

"But what's she like?" Des asked, like I was leaving out crucial information.

And maybe I was. Because it was hard to describe April to someone who didn't already know her. "She's... complicated." I said at last.

"And here I thought you'd want a low-maintenance kind of girl."

"I wouldn't call her high maintenance."

"No?"

I took a breath, knowing I was flubbing this up. I changed out of my shorts and into slacks, knowing Des had seen it all a thousand times before, and then I sat on my desk chair, meeting my sister's gaze.

"She's the kind of rain you get after months of a drought. Refreshing, harsh, all-consuming. Different."

My sister's lips quirked at the corners. "Sounds like my kind of girl."

While I finished changing and styling my hair, Des and I caught up. She had driven into town to see me off before my last homecoming and would be flying out of LA the next morning to do another performance with Jude. There were talks of an international tour in the works, and I could just picture Des performing in Paris, Rome, Prague. All the destinations she'd been bold enough to dream of.

When we went upstairs, Dad was home from work. He told me I looked good, and Mom fussed over my curls before giving up. Adelita and Marisol gave me hugs, Mateo seemed unimpressed, and we all posed for a siblings picture while Mom took way too many shots, "just in case."

"Are you going to pick her up?" Des asked.

I shook my head. "I'm meeting her and her friend at the dance."

"Have fun," she said, echoed by my parents. The younger three had already disappeared, probably back to their video game. I hugged my parents and big sister, then got in my car, driving toward the school.

Nerves had my hands tapping on the steering wheel as I drove. This was my first big date with April. The first time we'd dress up together. The first time I'd get to hold her close and spin her around the dance floor. I couldn't imagine anything better.

So, when I parked my car at the school, where

we'd be having the dance in the gymnasium, I didn't waste any time in my car. I took the corsage out of the package and went to the front bench, waiting for her and Sadie as other couples went into the school.

Unlike prom, anyone could go to homecoming, and as a few freshmen walked past me, it struck me how young they looked.

Only three years ago, I'd been in their place— hanging out with my friends, going to my first homecoming dance. But tonight was my last, and I wanted it to be one to remember.

A fancy limo pulled up, and I wondered who at school would have rented a limo for homecoming. That was until I saw the quarterback from Brentwood Academy get out of the limo and hold Kenzie's hand as she followed.

She looked pretty in a red dress, and the quarterback couldn't take his eyes off of her. Deena and another guy I recognized from Brentwood followed them out.

"Hey, Kenz, Deena!" I said, drawing their attention as they got closer. "You two look great."

"Thanks," Kenzie said, grinning from ear to ear. I hadn't seen her this happy in so long. "This is

Baxter, and his friend Pierre came along to go with Deena."

I waved at the guys, and they nodded my way. "Hope you all have a good time."

"We will," Kenzie said, sending a smile my way. "Save me a dance if you can peel yourself away from April."

"Unlikely," I retorted with a grin before they went into the building.

And as soon as I saw April walking toward me, I knew it would be more than unlikely. It would be impossible.

She wore this beautiful *mauve* dress with gauzy fabric that wrapped around her curves and swayed around her legs as she walked. Her heels gave her hips an extra swing, and I'd be lying if I said I wasn't completely mesmerized.

Even better was her smile. She wore dark lipstick that made her full lips the center of attention, followed by her eyes. All wide and blue and pretty.

"You look amazing," I breathed when she got close enough to hear me.

Her cheeks got that adorable pink tinge to them. "You look good too, Diego."

I almost didn't realize that Sadie was walking beside her until she said, "I'll see you two inside." She gave us a knowing smile before walking toward the school, the sun catching on the sequins of her black dress and the buckles of her black chunky boots.

I took April's hand and lifted it so she'd spin. As she did, I drank in every last drop of her. "Beautiful."

She shook her head slightly. "If you keep complimenting me, my head won't fit through the door."

"Then we should get you inside so I can compliment you more," I teased. "Because I am the luckiest guy here tonight."

And I meant it. Every last word.

"I GOT THIS FOR YOU," Diego said. His eyes were honey in the light of the setting sun, his smile just as sweet as he held out a stunning corsage.

"Diego, it's beautiful," I breathed, staring at the arrangement. I'd been to a school dance or two, but no one had ever gotten me flowers. No one had ever made me feel as pretty as Diego had.

"Can I put it on you?" he asked.

Nodding, I extended my hand. He slipped the stretchy band over my wrist, and I stared at the flowers, the accents that perfectly matched my dress. This must be what girls feel like with their engagement rings. All giddy and just wanting to stare at it. "I love it. Thank you."

He bent, easily kissing me, and then pulled back. "You're welcome."

I could have stood in front of the school for hours, just kissing him, but he put his arm around me and walked with me toward the stairs. We took them slowly since I had to be careful in my heels, and then continued down the hallway.

The entire school had been decked out for homecoming, from blue and white balloon arches to giant hand-painted signs. But nothing had been transformed quite like the gym.

The hardwood floors were covered with a dark blue vinyl, and white gossamer streamed from the ceiling, giving the place a dreamy effect. A few tables sat off to one side of the gym and chairs lined the other. All the lighting had been dimmed, replaced only by a disco ball in the center of the dance floor and strobe lights flashing from the DJ stand.

"Do all dances here look this amazing?" I asked Diego.

He leaned closer, speaking in my ear so I could hear him above the music. "Just wait until you see prom."

I loved the insinuation in his voice—that we'd be going to prom together. Never before had I been so confident in future plans, but I knew, as long as I went to this school, I'd want Diego to be my date. Just so I could see him smiling at me the way he had as I'd approached him from the parking lot moments ago.

A slow song began playing over the speakers, and Diego said, "Can I have this dance?"

And for a moment, I wasn't a girl who knew how to leave more than how to stay. I was Diego's girlfriend, a princess ready to be swept into his arms. So I nodded and held on to the moment for as long as I possibly could.

He twirled me again, like he had in front of the school, but this time, he spun me back to his chest. He slid my hand to his shoulder, and I held on to his other hand, letting him lead the way as we slowly swayed to the music.

Diego spoke against my ear. "You know what's amazing?"

"What?" I asked, closing my eyes so I could savor this moment.

"The fact that you've been all over the world, lived in so many different states, and now, in this moment, you're here with me. You could have been anywhere else."

He was right.

So many pieces of my life had fallen apart when my dad got injured. And those pieces could have taken us anywhere. I shuddered to think what would have happened to us if Mom hadn't gotten her business off the ground, giving us the capability to live here and give Dad the care he deserved. And no matter how much I tried not to get attached to people or places... I was glad we'd landed here.

Emerson felt like home, more than any other place had.

I'd always thought the Kansas state motto was inspiring. *To the stars through difficulty.* I used to think it meant to keep pushing forward, no matter what obstacles stood in your way. Now I knew it meant something else.

It meant that no matter what difficulty lay in your past, something beautiful, something good, could always come out of it.

Diego and Sadie... they were my stars, lighting my sky no matter how difficult life felt.

"I'm glad I'm here with you," I said to Diego, my throat feeling thick with emotion

"I am too." His lips brushed my cheek, sending goosebumps down my arms.

The music changed to an upbeat song, and I searched the edges of the gym for Sadie. I expected to see her at one of the tables or maybe sitting in one of the chairs lining the wall. Instead, I saw her stepping away from Diego's friend Terrell.

Biting back my shock, I waved her over. "Let's dance!"

To my surprise, she came my way without any begging or pleading. At first, Sadie rocked back and forth, out of rhythm, her cheeks a bright pink. But eventually, she let go, a smile lifting her lips and the music making her swing her arms and hips. I didn't have much more rhythm than her, but Diego had enough for all three of us.

He smiled and laughed and danced, and it was like we were enveloped in his bubble. As the song ended, Diego took my hand. "Come here. I want to show you something."

Confused, I followed him off the dance floor. "Where are we going?"

We reached the corner of the gym, and he held up a finger. "In three, two..."

A loud crash sounded on the opposite side of the gym, confetti raining down from the ceiling. The chaperone standing at this side of the dance floor jogged over to find the source, but I could already tell.

Terrell and Xander held massive confetti poppers and sported matching devilish grins.

I playfully hit his chest. "You're sneaky!"

"I just know what I want," he teased, pulling me down the stairs into the locker room where Sadie and I always ate lunch. It was completely dark, and I was about to search the walls for the light switch when his phone light came on.

"I have something to show you," he said.

Confused, I followed him through the locker room to the opposite wall lined with lockers. He reached one and said, "Hold this light, will you?"

I nodded, holding the phone so the light shone on the combination. When he opened it, my mouth fell open. The entire floor-to-head-height locker had been filled to the brim with every kind of snack and drink we could wish for. I stared at a pink machine on the bottom shelf. "Is that..."

"A mini fridge?" he finished. "It's battery powered too. The battery pack will last a week. I bought an extra so you can change it out."

I reached out, touching a bag of chips. It was like a little convenience store for Sadie and me.

"Diego, this is.... amazing," I said, lowering his phone to a concrete bench so it cast a dim glow around the room. "How did you even get in here to do it?"

A light shined in his eyes. "Had some help."

He'd put so much effort into this... for me. "You didn't have to do all this."

He took my hands, lifting them so our palms pressed together. There was the most adorable smile on his face as he said, "I know this is your special place with Sadie. I wanted to make it even better."

My heart completely melted, and I moved my hands from his to frame his face, drawing him down for a kiss.

So much of my life for the last three years had been about my dad, my mom, making their lives run smoothly. Diego had given me so much more than a stash of snacks.

He'd given me something just for me. Not because I needed it, but because he wanted to make my life better. If only he knew he already had.

GETTING Coach Ripley to give me a locker in girls' locker room, using my surf lesson money to buy the snacks and a battery-powered refrigerator, having Kenzie stand guard so I could do it all without anyone coming in—it was all worth it. Just to see April smile like that.

It had been like she smiled with her entire heart, the light shining from her eyes and pouring through her lips. She kissed me like I'd given her so much more than what I had. And I kissed her back because I wanted her to know how special she was. How real this was to me. She wasn't like any other girl, and these feelings I had? They were like nothing I'd felt before.

Finally, I could understand how my sister could

pour her feelings out for a famous pop star on stage, despite backlash from the media and all his fans. I could see what kept my parents together through twenty-four years and five children. I could see myself dreaming of the future in ways I never had before.

April had done that for me.

This little gift? It was nothing in comparison.

When Terrell texted me the all-clear, I brought her out of the locker room, and we went back to the gym, spending minutes, hours, dancing together. Enjoying each other's company. Learning about each other.

Her favorite flower? Violets.

Her favorite movie? *The Secret Life of Walter Mitty*.

Her favorite food? Chili and cinnamon rolls. (Apparently that was a Kansas thing.)

I told her about my lessons with Jacinda, how I was still trying to come up with a good mission statement for my future business. I talked about how annoyed I used to get that Mateo copied my every move or that Adelita and Marisol fought over clothes in the morning. I shared how much I loved my family, and how someday, I wanted a family just like mine.

We talked about how fast senior year was going and how we couldn't believe our final CNA class was next week...

And then her phone began to ring.

She'd carried it with her in this wrist purse that matched her dress. But instead of putting her phone on silent, she excused herself, walking away from the dance floor to answer it.

I didn't feel great, standing there with everyone watching while my girl just walked away. So I followed her to the hallway right outside the gym and listened to what phone call was so important.

"Mom, slow down," she said. Then she nodded, her dark eyebrows drawn tightly together.

"Where is he?" she asked.

Another pause.

"Have you called the police?"

My chest tightened. This sounded really bad. I could hear a voice talking on the other end but couldn't make out the words.

"I haven't heard from him." She paused. "No, no texts or missed calls. I'm coming home."

April's expression pinched even more. "Yes, of course I'm coming home!... You think I could enjoy the dance with my dad missing?... I'll figure it out... Bye... Love you."

She hung up, turning toward me with tears already filling her eyes. "My dad is missing."

I covered my mouth. "April..."

"He took the car, and Mom doesn't know where he went."

My stomach sank, feeling her fear become my own. "Can he drive with his injury?"

"He's not supposed to because he's prone to seizures, but Mom's hoping his instincts will kick in." She shook her head, tears spilling down her cheeks. "I'm sorry, Diego. You can stay at the dance, but I need to go home."

"Didn't Sadie drive you?" I asked.

"I'll call a taxi. Mom will pay for it when I get there."

"Don't be ridiculous." I took her hand, holding on tightly. "I'll take you home."

Her eyes were wide blue pools as she looked up to me. "It's your senior homecoming, Diego. I've only been here a few months. This school—it's been your life."

I shook my head, shocked that she was thinking about me in a moment like this. "I've been to three homecoming dances, and most of this one. The only way I'd be missing out was if I wasn't there for you right now." I tilted my head. "Now come on, maybe we can look for him on the way to your house."

She bit her lip, nodding, and followed me down the hallway. We let go of each other's hands so she could hold her dress as we hurried down the stairs, and then we raced to my car in the parking lot.

I opened the door for her, holding it until she and all of her dress was inside, then jogged around to my side. I could see her knee shaking as we pulled out of the parking lot and drove toward our neighborhood.

"What car would he be driving?" I asked. "Yours or your mom's?"

"I didn't ask. God, I'm so stupid," she said, self-loathing in her voice.

"You're not stupid," I corrected. "It's just like the waves. Take a breath and swim through it."

She nodded, then said. "He'll either be in my maroon Toyota or Mom's black Hyundai. It's an SUV, and she has her toll pass in the front window."

"That's my girl," I said, searching out the front windshield for either of those makes or models. It was hard on the highway with it being so dark outside, but it got easier in the well-lit streets of our neighborhood. April kept her face pressed to the window, her skin looking pale against the dash lights and streetlights pouring through.

My phone went off loudly, along with April's. "What is it?" I asked.

She held the phone up, her voice shaky as she said, "Missing person alert. Man missing in a maroon Toyota Camry. Thirty-six years old. Six-four, brown eyes, brown hair. May be aggravated and confused."

Each word made my stomach turn.

When we got to her house, she jumped out of my car without a word, hurrying to her front door, and I followed her inside, needing to know that everything would be okay.

Her mom met us in the living room, holding both of April's arms. "I still don't have any new information, but they put out a missing person alert for him. Hopefully they'll be able to find him before something bad happens."

April's voice was steady, reassuring to her mom. "They'll find him, Mom. It'll be okay."

Her mom nodded, taking a deep breath, and then her eyes flicked toward me. "You must be Diego. I'm Grace. I'm so sorry to ruin your night."

So this was where April got it—the thoughtfulness. "My night's not ruined. I just hope we can find him. Do you want me to drive around the neighborhood?"

"Can you stay here with April so she's not alone?" Grace said. "I'll go out and see if I can find him at the gas station or somewhere close. Call me if he comes back."

There was worry in April's eyes, but I said, "Of course."

April nodded. "Be safe, Mom."

When Grace walked out the door, April said, "I'm going upstairs to change real fast. I'll be right back."

I nodded. "I'll be here." I sat on the couch for emphasis.

Her smile left just as quickly as it came before she turned and went up the stairs. While she was gone, I glanced around the living room, seeing this piece of her for the first time.

There weren't many decorations on the walls, but there was a big picture of April with her parents above the mantel, no glass in the frame. She looked younger here, maybe twelve or thirteen. Her mom looked younger too, less lines in her face. The man, her dad, had a strong face, square jaw, broad shoulders. He was a wall of a man between April and

Grace, with kind brown eyes and a short brown beard.

"That was right before Dad was deployed," April said.

I nearly jumped, not having heard her come down the stairs. But now she walked toward the photo, leggings hugging her curves and a big Army T-shirt hanging from her frame.

"Dad had been gone just a few months before he got injured. That's the last photo of the three of us before..." She let the words hang between us, because we both knew what she meant.

The last photo before their lives changed forever.

"Where do you think he is?" I asked.

She shook her head. "Sometimes I think he forgets he's injured, or he thinks he should just be able to go do what he wants. Usually, Mom can talk him out of it, but something must have happened tonight."

I hated to see the concern in her eyes. "I can tell how much you love him."

"I do," she breathed. "Sometimes I feel guilty for wishing things were different."

It was the closest she'd ever let me in, and I

could see the vulnerability in her posture, in the water falling from her eyes.

"Of course you do," I said softly, standing to put a hand on her back.

She stood still for less than a second before stepping away. "You don't have to stay here," she said. "You can go home if you want to. Maybe catch an after-party with Xander and Terrell."

I shook my head. "Did you hear your mom? She asked me to stay here with you."

"I'm fine," April argued, but her words were cut off by a knock on the door.

She hurried to the window, pulling aside sheer white curtains and revealing a police car in the driveway. I followed her to the front door, which she quickly pulled open.

Two officers stood with a shadow of the man I'd seen in the photo. He was still just as tall, but now his shoulders slumped. He was thinner, less brawny than before. There were pocks of scars on one side of his face and neck. His eyes flashed over me for only a moment before going back to the floor.

"Dad," April breathed. "I'm so glad you're okay."

"This is Douglas Adams?" the officer confirmed.

Her dad shoved off the officer. "'Course I am," he grunted, stumbling past the officers, past April and me, toward the kitchen. Now I noticed the shopping bags in his hands as he went to the kitchen, banging around in the cabinets. "I'm a grown man. I can go to the store," he grumbled loudly.

My heart rate picked up like I could feel a big wave approaching.

"He was at the store?" April asked.

The officer on the right nodded, speaking under a thick mustache. "We spotted the car, probably on his way back here from the store, and pulled him over. He was driving without a license, but we're going to let him go with a warning today."

"Thank you," April said, her voice sounding small. "Thank you so much."

The officer nodded, exchanging a glance with his shorter partner. "Be sure you keep those keys locked up in a secure place." He looked inside the door, tapping the beach-themed key rack with a thick finger. "This ain't gonna cut it anymore."

"Absolutely," April said, taking the keys from him. She slipped them in the pocket of her leggings.

A pan clattered loudly on the kitchen floor,

followed by a string of curse words from April's father.

The officers peered around us, the vocal one asking, "Are you sure you're okay, young lady?"

April nodded. "I'll be fine. Have you called my mom?"

He shook his head. "Why don't you do that and let her know he's home safe?"

"I will," April agreed.

The silent officer spoke up. "The vehicle's on the side of the road by mile marker fifty-one. Call us if you need anything, miss."

She nodded, slowly closing the door behind them, and then took out her phone to call her mom.

Their conversation was short and ended with a quick "I love you."

April held her phone to her chest. "Mom was just at the gas station. She'll be here in five."

"Good," I said. Another noise came from the kitchen, followed by the sound of cracking plastic.

"You should be good to go," April said, taking my hand and trying to pull me toward the door.

I stood firm and looked from the kitchen doorway to her eyes. "April, it's okay to let me in. You don't have to be embarrassed about this."

"OW!" her dad shouted from the kitchen. Her eyes widened as she hurried past me to see her dad putting his hand under the running faucet. He already had a nasty red burn mark on his arm.

"Dad, are you okay?" she asked.

He slammed the water off, making the faucet shake with his force. "I'm a grown man, April."

"I know that," she said gently, "I just—"

"This is ridiculous." He smacked his uninjured hand on the counter, walking closer to us.

I could feel April shrivel beside me, making herself as small as possible. Instinctively, I stepped between her and her dad.

His nostrils flared. "And who do you think you are?"

"I'm April's boyfriend," I said, not letting any hint of fear into my voice.

"No, you aren't," he snarled.

April tried to get around me, but I sidestepped, caging her back. I didn't like this for her. Not one bit.

"Get out of my house," he growled.

I held up my hand, trying to calm him. "I'll be on my way as soon as Mrs. Adams gets home and you cool down."

An angry mix of a roar and a shout ripped from

his mouth, his pupils shrinking so small I could barely see them in the brown of his eyes. "GET OUT OF MY HOUSE." He grabbed for my arm, pulling me and pinning me against the cabinet with all his weight.

"Dad!" April cried, the only thing I could hear over the splitting pain in my wrist.

Her dad spun me again, throwing me toward the back door, and then he rounded on April. "WHAT KIND OF LOWLIFE ARE YOU BRINGING INTO THIS HOUSE?" He screamed, shaking her shoulders.

White filled my vision and I reached for him, pulling him away and tackling him to the ground. He was strong, scrabbling beneath me. I held him in place, praying he would cool down, that this wouldn't get any worse.

The door opened, and Grace screamed, "Oh my god!"

"Mom! Help!" April yelled.

Her dad found purchase on my arm, making me cry out in pain, but I gritted through it, knowing this was just a wave. That all waves crashed to the ocean floor and eventually rolled away.

Grace hurried past us to the cabinet, pulling out

a glass medicine bottle and a syringe. She pulled off the cap, filling it with clear liquid.

"Hold still, Diego," Grace said, then plunged the needle into April's dad's shoulder. He struggled, letting loose a stream of curses, before his body slowly went limp beneath me.

I could taste bile in my mouth as I got up, eyes darting between April and her mom. April's shoulders shook with sobs, and she wrapped her arms around her waist.

I stepped toward her, wanting to comfort her, but she retreated, shaking her head.

"Go home, Diego."

"But—" I began.

"*Go*," she ordered, her voice as cold as her eyes had become.

The pain in my wrist, in my chest, bloomed, and I turned away, afraid I might be sick.

I went outside, taking assessment of my body. My shirt had been ripped, my hip had banged against the counter and was surely bruised. There was a serious chance my wrist was broken. But what hurt worst of all was knowing what could have happened to April if I hadn't been there. And the terrifying thought that my presence had made it all worse.

I had my hand on my car door when I heard a voice so similar to April's say, "Diego, wait."

I turned from the car, facing the woman who looked so much like her daughter.

"Honey, are you okay?" she asked, looking from my wrist to my face.

The care in her voice made a lump form in my throat. I swallowed it back, shaking my head. "He was shaking her and I just—I couldn't just stand back."

Her eyes were pools of blue compassion. "I know, honey."

"But April—" Emotion clogged my throat, blocking my words.

"Give her some time," she said.

And I nodded, because that was all I could bring myself to do.

## FORTY-FIVE

## DIEGO

I GOT IN MY CAR, holding my wrist tightly to my chest. It was only a couple minutes to drive home, but each bump of the road sent pain slicing through my arm. It was no match for the lump growing in my throat, the dread settling in my stomach.

I'd seen the way April had looked at me. Felt the fight leave her dad's body. This wasn't something you got over. It was something that ended everything.

I pulled up the house, the light still on over the kitchen window. My sister's car was in the driveway. I leaned my head back against the seat, fighting hot tears.

Everything about this night had gone so wrong.

I'd told April this relationship could be different.

And I'd hoped she would move forward. With me. It turned out every fear was true. I could feel her slipping away before she even said a word.

I saw a face appear in the window, my sister, waving me in.

But I couldn't bring myself to do it. So I called my mom.

"*Bueno*," she said, sounding slightly confused.

My voice cracked. "*Necesito ir al doctor.*" *I need to go to the doctor.*

"*¿Estás bien?*" *Are you okay?*

My throat constricted. "No." Not even close.

## FORTY-SIX

## APRIL

MOM SLEPT in my bed with me. Or rather, she slept. I lay awake, my eyes aching from the sting of tears. My mind just kept replaying the scene over and over again. How Diego had stepped in front of me, trying to defend me, not knowing he was only escalating the situation.

Then to see my dad, the strongest person I'd ever known, held down by the guy I was falling for... a fresh wave of hot tears began, soothing my irritated eyes and burning everything else.

Mom had only used that sedative four times in the last three years, and I brought someone into our home who made her use it the fifth.

It wasn't Diego's fault, not really. It was mine.

There were a million ways tonight could have

ended differently. Maybe I could have warned Diego about some of Dad's triggers. Insisted he leave the house. Never brought him home in the first place.

But that only would have helped tonight.

I'd forgotten who I was. Shunned my responsibilities and pretended I could be a regular girl, when reality was so much different. I knew everything in life had an end, and yet I'd let myself hope for something that would last.

I could hear my phone vibrating with notifications from Diego, from Sadie. But I let them go. I couldn't bear to fool myself anymore that those relationships could last.

So I did what I did best. I left. I left without going anywhere at all.

## FORTY-SEVEN

I WAITED OUTSIDE THE SCHOOL, my arm in a cast and a sling.

I wished I could disappear. Stay home so I wouldn't face questions about my arm from guys on the football team who were counting on me. But I had to see April. I waved off a few teammates with short answers. But then Xander approached, his hair as messy as the papers he was shoving into his backpack.

"Diego—what happened?" He stopped a foot away, scanning my arm.

I shook my head, my jaw clenched. "Don't want to talk about it."

"But football—" he began.

I cut him off. "I can't play anymore, Xander. I'm done for the season."

His jaw went slack. "It's broken?"

I barely shifted my chin as a fresh wave of regret washed over me. When the ER doctor told me I'd be in a cast for the next six weeks, at least, I knew it was over. All the fun I'd planned on having my senior year... the playoffs, maybe a state championship played with my best friends, gone in an instant.

But still I worried about April. Her dad had been so aggravated. Would he retaliate after that medicine Grace gave him? Were they both okay? How had they made it three years with those kind of blowups in their home?

Over Xander's shoulder, I spotted April walking through the parking lot, her eyes on the asphalt.

"I gotta go," I said, pushing past Xander toward my girl. I searched her body, looking for any hint of injury after I'd left. She'd mentioned things being hard with her dad, but never the temper that came with his trauma.

"April," I breathed, stepping up to her.

She looked up at me, dark circles under her eyes like she hadn't slept since I'd left. Life only came to her gaze when her eyes landed on my cast. Her full lips parted. "Your wrist."

"It's broken," I finished flatly. I didn't care about me right now. "Is everything okay at home? Is your dad okay?"

"Broken?" was all she said, her arms folded across her chest like she was trying to hold herself together.

I reached out to touch her shoulders, comfort her, but she stepped away.

It was worse than a slap to the face.

Worse than any mean words she could have said.

"April," I breathed.

She shook her head, her eyes already shining with moisture. "I told you this would happen."

"That what would happen?" I asked. "You were in a crisis, and I was there. I told you I'd be there."

Her voice rose. "My dad had to be sedated! He *broke your arm*!"

I could feel people around us staring, but I didn't care about them. I had lost one of the best parts of school. I couldn't lose April too. "Accidents happen, April. That doesn't mean we shouldn't be together."

She stepped back, staring into my eyes with hers

full of pain. "Accidents? You're in a cast! You should have been at homecoming."

I pressed my lips together, desperate for a way to make her understand. "You can't surf a wave without having some scary moments sometimes."

"This isn't surfing," she said sadly. "This is my life. And there's no getting back on the board. Not when it comes to us."

My throat tightened. "April, it doesn't have to be like this."

"But it is." She pushed past me, and I turned, holding my hand over my mouth as I watched her go to the school steps. Walking toward the arch that said *Ad Meliora*.

I just never thought better things for her would mean walking away from me.

## FORTY-EIGHT

## APRIL

I DIDN'T WANT to be here.

Not in this school. Not in this town.

Not in this moment that felt like fire consuming everything I thought I loved.

But that was the life of a military brat. We didn't choose where we moved. We just did. We got along. Made friends. Blended in until it was time for another move.

But Mom had decided this was the place for Dad. And I didn't know how I could stay here when every place I passed held so many memories of Diego. He'd walked me to every class. Carried all of my books. Worn my backpack so easily over his broad shoulders. Held my hand so securely in his own.

I'd never see those hands without knowing they were the same hands that had wrestled my dad to the ground.

Diego had been trying to defend me—I knew that deep down—but it didn't change the images in my mind that appeared every time I closed my eyes.

Finally, the lunch bell rang, and I hurried to the locker room, not even bothering to bring a tray. I just needed some peace—some time away from every student aiming their silent questions at me. I felt like they could see my guilt like a sash across my chest.

*That's the girl who ruined Diego De Leon's senior year.*

I reached the bottom of the steps, and my eyes immediately landed on the locker.

The one Diego had shown me during homecoming.

I covered my mouth, a lump forming in my throat.

I'd forgotten the gift he'd prepared for Sadie and me. And it made my heart fracture that much more. Diego was the dream boyfriend. He'd done so much for me. And I'd ruined everything, just like I knew I would.

"April," Sadie said from the stairs.

I turned to face her, seeing a confused look on her face.

"What happened to Diego's arm?"

Guilt wracked through me, slicing like a hot knife. I blinked quickly, looking away.

"Did something happen after homecoming? I thought maybe you and Diego just skipped out and forgot to tell me you were leaving..."

My gut clenched with even more guilt. I'd left my so-called best friend at the dance without so much as a text explaining why I had to leave. I was *so* selfish. I couldn't sit with myself, much less Sadie, or I'd implode. "I just can't right now. Okay?"

"What do you mean?" she asked.

Why was it so hard to get my point across? "I need some space, Sadie."

Hurt, confusion, both emotions crashed across her face. "Did I do something?"

My chest ached. "No. I did."

Then I walked out to the parking lot to go home, because I knew I couldn't make it through another second here.

I pulled up to the house, seeing Mom's car out front, and breathed a sigh of relief.

My mom was more than my best friend. She was the person who understood all of this better than anyone else.

I got out of my car, leaving my backpack in the back seat, and went to the front door. But when I got inside, I didn't see Mom in the living room or kitchen where she usually worked with her laptop while Dad went about his day.

"Mom?" I called out.

"April? Is that you?" she yelled back, coming out of Dad's room.

Confused, I looked over her shoulder. Dad's room was a mess, filled with suitcases and his clothing strewn all over the place.

I walked past her, my eyebrows drawing together as I took in the scene. My brain couldn't quite piece it together. "Are you cleaning?"

"April, I—" she began, but then her voice faded as I stepped through the doorway.

Every dresser drawer had been pulled out and emptied. No more clothes hung in his closet, aside from his old dress uniform.

I turned back to face Mom, my silent question

taking up space between us. It suffocated me, sucking all the air from the room, from my lungs.

When she wouldn't meet my eyes, I knew. But I still hoped for something different. "Is he taking a different room?"

Mom slowly shook her head.

"Then what?" I asked, needing to hear her say it.

Her chest heaved with a heavy breath. "He's going to live at the center."

I crumbled to his freshly made bed. *At the center*, she'd said. Like she wasn't moving him to an institution. A home.

That brochure sat in my backpack, heavier than ever. Despite the weight of Dad's care, I'd never taken it out. Never suggested it to Mom. I never imagined she could make this kind of decision without even consulting me.

"April, honey, I—"

I held up my hand, unable to take another blow. "Stop."

She fell silent, standing just feet away from me.

My heart could hardly beat through each pulse of my shattered heart.

After the room stop spinning, I looked up at her, seeing her worry lines, the wrinkles, the circles under her eyes clearer than ever. "How could you do this without telling me?"

"Because I knew you'd talk me out of it." She wasn't sad, apologetic. Only honest.

"We can't do this to him," I breathed. "After everything he's sacrificed for us?"

"We should have done it sooner."

I shook my head, embers of anger blooming in my chest. "How could you say that?"

"Because he was going to hurt you," Mom said, her voice trembling. "He hurt Diego. He ran away! It's not safe to have him here without support."

"Mom—" I began to argue, but she shook her head.

"You need to hear me. All of what I have to say."

I wanted to argue, but I clenched my jaw to hold it in.

"Your father gave so much for this family, this country." Her voice choked up. "But we've been sacrificing for him for three years. We've taken classes and gotten help, and even with all that information and practice, what we're doing *isn't good enough*. And if your father knew, before his accident, that he'd put you and your boyfriend at risk, he would want me to make this decision. I know he would. This isn't a good situation. Not for him, and not for us either."

Emotion flowed through my eyes and slipped down my cheeks. I shook my head, wanting to argue with her. Wanting to find a way to beg for him to stay.

But the truth hurt just as much.

Our lives would be so much *easier* without having to worry about the next time he'd fly off the handle or leave without us knowing.

It felt wrong to admit that. Wrong to accept it. "Dad's leaving?" My voice shattered on the words.

Mom closed the distance between us, and this time, I didn't shy away. I sobbed into her chest as she smoothed the hair at the back of my neck. "Your father deserves to be somewhere that knows how to care for him, with people who won't grow to resent him."

A sob left my throat at the gut punch of the truth. I was mad at Dad for what he'd done to Diego. What I'd lost as a result. It wasn't Dad's fault that he had an injury, a disability that affected his behavior. But I was angry. Devastated. I didn't want to be mad at Dad for what I'd lost the last three years, but I could feel it in the pit of my stomach like a poison. "I feel so *guilty*," I admitted. "Like we failed him."

She took my face in her hands, my tears soaking her fingers. "Your dad will always be your dad. He'll always be my husband. Whether he lives under this roof or not. And you can love him without giving up all of yourself."

The problem was, I didn't know how.

## FORTY-NINE

## DIEGO

I HADN'T TOLD Coach Ripley what happened after homecoming, and I was dreading each second, every step to the football field.

I skipped the locker room and walked down the well-worn path between the school and the field. Some girls walked around me, chirping, "Hey, Diego." "Sorry about your arm." "I want to sign your cast sometime" as they went.

I managed to send a smile their way, but inside, I was being ripped apart. Step by step.

All too soon, I reached the field. Without thinking, I glanced to the spot in the stands where April always sat. She'd looked so cute during the homecoming game, my number drawn on her cheek with a face paint pen, holding up a glitter sign just for me. Sadie had sat beside her, her turquoise hair just as bright as the stadium lights.

I thought back to the homecoming game. Had I enjoyed it enough? Would I have played differently if I'd known it would be my last game?

Coach Ripley and assistant coach Bryon stood by the water coolers. Ripley stood like he always did. Arms folded across his chest, feet just slightly farther than shoulder width distance apart, chin pulled back, and a serious look on his face as he spoke with Bryon.

"Coach," I said, my voice steady despite how weak I felt inside.

Both men turned my way. While Ripley's jaw clenched, Bryon's lips parted.

"What the hell happened?" Ripley said, no tact.

He was going to make me say it.

I held out my cast. "My wrist is broken. I'm out for six weeks."

Ripley's jaw clenched some more. "That's the rest of the season."

"Yessir."

Bryon looked between Ripley and me.

Without even meeting my eyes, Ripley said, "You'll still come to games and practices, pass out water and towels with the manager."

It was another punch to the gut. A demotion for something I couldn't control. And the only thing worse than being injured and unable to play? Sitting on the sidelines and watching everyone else do what I could not.

When I didn't move, Ripley said, "Is there an issue, son?"

I was about to shake my head, but I had nothing left to lose. "I can't."

"Your other arm is okay, right?" he said.

I put my hand over my chest. "But I'm not."

Bryon twisted his lips to the side. Just the hint of humanity I needed.

"I just found out I'm out for my last year of football. My girlfriend broke up with me. I don't know what I'm doing next, and I'm feeling... lost." My voice broke on the last word.

Ripley and Bryon exchanged a glance, then Ripley nodded. Bryon walked away and Coach came toward me, putting his arm around my shoulders. He walked with me, toward the corner of the field, quiet for a few steps. "You take a few days to grieve, and then you come back here to practice."

I stared at him. Did he really not hear a word I just said?

He cleared his throat. "Football only lasts four

years, if we're lucky. Each year, we get a new crop of freshmen, ready to make their mark. And we say goodbye to seniors. Some are easier to say goodbye to than others. I'm not quite ready to say goodbye to you yet, Diego."

I met his eyes, full of emotion for the first time.

My tongue felt thick as I nodded. "Yessir."

MOM and I walked down the tiled halls with Dr. Sanders toward Dad's new suite. Earlier that day, at the center, she'd sat with Dr. Sanders and made plans, then went to lunch with Dad and the doctor, telling him the news.

Mom said it had been hard, but in his way, he understood.

Now we were bringing his things to unpack. Mom pushed the rolling cart piled with bags and boxes.

Dr. Sanders slowed at a door. There was a temporary sign printed on white paper taped over the cherry-colored wood.

ROOM 204

## Douglas Adams

Mom and I glanced at each other. She reached for my hand, and I held hers back. Tight.

I couldn't help but think of surfing with Diego. Swimming under another wave.

And even though it felt like all I would do was tumble and drown under the surface of roiling waves, her hand was a tug of the leash.

A reminder.

*I've got you, April.*

Dr. Sanders knocked, and for a long moment, I thought Dad might ignore us, so angry by this move. Instead, he said, "Come in."

She pushed the door open, and my heart ached, swelled, as we took it all in. The floor was bright white tile, bouncing back sunshine from the wall full of windows on the opposite side of the room that overlooked the pond between the center and the hospital. There was a couch, a television. Even a little kitchenette. No burner, but he had a small refrigerator for snacks and a sink and ice maker.

"Douglas?" Dr. Sanders called out.

Dad stepped out of a doorway I assumed led to

his bedroom. With the light bouncing off him and his injury not visible from this angle, I could almost see him as my old dad. Or maybe even a newer version of the one I had.

A dad who would be cared for in a way Mom and I couldn't. He'd have other people here, support and understanding we couldn't offer. And the best part was, we could visit any time, with staff around for assistance in case we ever needed it.

Mom stopped the luggage cart and stepped beside it. "What do you think of it, Doug?"

He scratched his neck, looking around. "I like it. Nice enough for you to come visit?"

"Oh, Doug," she said, going into his arms for a hug.

He looked up at me, exhaustion in his eyes, and waved me over. "Get over here, monkey."

Tears fell down my cheeks as I went to him.

In their arms, for the first time, I didn't imagine or pretend that this was my old dad and my old life.

No, instead I savored this new family. It wasn't perfect, not even close. There was so much more I wished I could do for both of my parents. But despite all the odds, we were here. And we still had each other.

And in the end, that had to be enough.

## FIFTY-ONE
## DIEGO

I WALKED INTO ETC, prepared but not ready to take my CNA exam. For the last seven weeks, April and I had gone through the class, turned in our homework, and changed so much in the process.

But this chapter? It was coming to a close.

Instead of going to the classroom we usually did, we followed Janice to the computer lab, already set up for our exam.

I could feel the electricity in the room when April walked in. From the dull ache in my chest to the electricity that crackled across my skin. But I had to accept that healing happened at different paces. That if she wasn't ready, I couldn't force her to be.

No matter how much I wished I could.

So I focused on my computer screen, answering questions we'd gone over in class. Before I knew it, I'd reached the last question.

Janice came up behind me, patting my shoulder. "Good job, Diego. You'll have your results in a couple weeks." She handed me an envelope. "This is your assignment with Emerson Acres to get your clinical hours in. They've worked it out so you can do it during your school's volunteer time."

I nodded, feeling a sense of finality come over me.

April wouldn't be coming over to my house anymore, and since we only had first hour together and didn't run in overlapping circles, I'd hardly see her at school. She could walk Heidi in another direction.

We were over.

*Over.*

My breath felt ragged as it passed through my lips. My heart felt torn.

But I got in my car and drove to the school for the football game, because I was a member of the team. My friends, my coach wanted me there.

When I took my position by the water coolers, I glanced toward the stands.

And there was my family, holding up a sign that said: We <3 Diego.

And I felt it, just like that tug I'd given April at the lesson, saying they'd be there for me. That I wasn't alone.

And that somehow, no matter how much this hurt, I'd make it through to ride another wave.

## FIFTY-TWO

## SADIE

I'VE NEVER BEEN the kind of girl who has friends.

In fact, I'm the kind of girl who doesn't.

So I didn't expect to like April as much as I did. I didn't plan to like having her company during lunch or enjoy getting milkshakes at Waldo's after football games.

But this Friday, sitting at my parents' pottery studio with a lump of clay spinning between my hands, I knew something was missing. Even before my mom unplugged my pottery wheel and said, "We need to talk."

I wished my hands weren't wet and muddy so I could plug the wheel back in and ignore her comment altogether. But Mom wasn't moving. And she was holding out a wet rag for me to wipe off my hands.

I took the rag, wiping between my fingers, and heard a chair scrape over the floor. Dad was coming over too. The three of us were sitting in a triangle like they thought they were hosting some kind of intervention.

I let out a sigh, my eyes already stinging as I mumbled, "Can we just *say* we had this talk and move on?"

Dad chuckled quietly. "I wish, kiddo."

Mom leaned forward on her chair, her elbows resting on her knees. "The football season's going to be over before you know it."

I raised my eyebrows. That was the last thing I'd expected to hear.

"And you haven't been to a game since home-coming," Mom said. "That's two games gone that you'll never get back."

"You've been keeping track?" I asked.

Dad raised his hand. "Me actually. You know your mom's terrible with tracking time. It's her creative brain."

Mom nodded. "I knew it had been awhile, but Dad said it's been two weeks since you gone out with April after school, honey. Is everything okay?"

They knew it wasn't. Otherwise we wouldn't be having this sit-down. "If I tell you it's okay, can I go back to making this vase? I think I can sell it as 'abstract art.'"

My parents smiled at each other, but it didn't last long before Dad said, "We've always let you do your own thing, be your own person, but we've also seen so much growth in you this year. You've been stepping outside of your shell, experiencing life instead of watching it. And we want to at least understand what happened, even if we can't help."

I looked between my parents. Dad in his big and tall overalls covered in clay and paint. Mom in her sweatshirt and jeans. Both of them wearing matching concern in their eyes. I used to be able to talk to them about my life, but I didn't understand what was going on myself. How could I explain it to them?

My mom reached across our circle, putting her hand on my knee. "You can tell us whatever it is. We won't judge you."

I let out a little sigh, looking at my hands in my lap. There was still red in the creases of my palm and fingers from the clay. "Honestly? I don't really know what happened. April and I had a great time at homecoming, and then all of a sudden, she was gone. I thought maybe she left with her boyfriend, but then when I saw her at school, she told me she wanted space." My voice felt rough, and I wiped at my tingling nose. "She hasn't eaten lunch with me since then, or even texted, and I don't know what to do."

"Oh, honey," Mom said.

Dad grumbled. His typical response to anyone wronging me in any way.

Mom said, "When you and April were in the dressing rooms, her mom, Grace, told me how special it was that April had a friend. They've moved around her entire life, and I think April is somewhat of a loner. Maybe things got too real?"

Now my eyes were full-on watering, because things had been real for me too. I loved having April as a friend, having someone to talk to. I'd even considered confiding in her about the guy I had a crush on. "So she just disappeared? How is that right?"

"It's not right," Mom said, to Dad's effusive nodding. "But relationships all have dips. If you think it's a relationship worth keeping, you have to get to the other side of the down so you can have an up as well."

I bit my lip. This was all new to me. "How do I do something like that?"

Mom and Dad exchanged a glance, and Dad said, "Sometimes you have to extend an olive branch."

"Where do I get one of those?"

Both of my parents laughed, making my cheeks heat. I wasn't the greatest with metaphor.

Dad said, "It's a figure of speech. You can extend something that shows you're on her side and you care about her happiness."

Mom nodded. "And if she's a friend worth having, she'll accept the branch and learn that freezing you out, even if she's struggling, isn't okay."

After a few moments, I said, "I need to think about it. So will you let me finish my abstract art?"

Mom came to me, hugging me, and said, "Oh, honey, everything you make is abstract."

LAST NIGHT, it came to me.

My mission.

The purpose I'd been waiting for that would make the risk of going all in with my business worth it.

So I packed up my computer Saturday morning and went to Seaton Bakery before my next meeting with Jacinda Junco. After ordering breakfast, I sat in a corner booth and started typing with my good hand.

### Diego's Surf School

Mission Statement

Surfing teaches you so many things you can't learn
in school.
I've never sat in a classroom and felt powerful,
strong, energized, and refreshed.
But I've felt that way on a surfboard, facing the
rolling curve of a wave.
In school, you pass or fail.
But on the board, you practice.
And when you stand on the board and ride a
wave...
You're free to enjoy the ride. And you have to live in
the moment, because if you spend too much time
thinking about the last wipeout or the next wave,
you'll miss the magic of the moment.
And even if this moment is a painful one, you know
you'll be okay, because there's always another
chance to get up and ride again.

I sat back, looking at the words on my computer screen. They weren't pretty or poetic, but they were the truest thing I knew.

Feeling a sense of release, of peace but also of purpose, I relaxed and ate my breakfast until

Jacinda came into the bakery. She waved at me and then ordered breakfast.

My heart beat quickly with nerves, because I knew this was it. If Jacinda didn't think this was good enough, I didn't have any more to offer.

It felt like forever until she was walking my way with coffee and a donut in hand. "Looks like you've been hard at work," she said, nodding at my computer before setting down her food and drink.

"I have," I said, trying to keep calm. "I'm excited to hear what you think about my mission statement."

Her eyes lit up with excitement. "Can you show me?"

I nodded, spinning the computer on the table so she could see it.

She scanned the computer, her eyes tracking back and forth over the words until a smile slowly formed on her lips. She tapped the track pad with her finger and turned it toward me, with a new line typed and highlighted at the bottom of the page.

"Diego, this is your motto."

I stared at the words, hardly believing they were mine, but feeling them on a deep soul level.

*Enjoy the magic of the moment.*

My throat got tight, as I realized I'd done that with April. I'd enjoyed every second I had with her. That was all I could do.

Jacinda's voice almost startled me out of my thoughts. "Are you ready for all the work this is going to take?"

I cleared the emotion from my throat. "Absolutely."

Jacinda and I worked in the bakery for hours, creating a business plan for Diego's Surf School. I was mentally tired, but happy I had an entire document on my computer dedicated to creating a life I wanted to live. One where I could truly enjoy the moment.

We agreed to meet again the next weekend, and then I left, getting in my car. I was about to call Xander and Terrell to see if they wanted to hit the skate park when a call from a number I didn't recognize came through the speaker system.

I got calls every so often from flyers I had around town for surf lessons, so I hit the button on the dash to answer the call. "Hi, this is Diego," I said.

"Diego? It's Sadie."

My heart lurched with her name. She and April had been so close, but for the last few weeks, April had been eating lunch in the cafeteria alone. "Uh, hi, Sadie. What's up?"

"I... was hoping you'd give me a surf lesson?"

That was even more surprising than getting a call from her. "You want to learn to surf?" She really didn't seem like the surfing type.

"Yeah, my parents want me to have more extracurricular activities, and I thought of you. I hope that's okay. I know you and April are off but—"

"It's totally fine," I said, not wanting to dig up even more pain. "I can't really do much in the water with my wrist."

"But we can do some practicing on shore, right?" she asked.

"Yeah, I mean, it is easier to stand in the water once you get your form down on land..." And I was excited to give a surf lesson now that I had my official mission and motto in place. "I'm free in a couple hours if you want to come over?"

"Oh, today?" she asked, seeming happily surprised but also nervous.

"Yeah, if it works for you," I said.

"Right. Today is good. I'll see you around..."

"Four should be good," I said.

"Four it is."

I CAME home from eating lunch with Dad at the Rhodora Center and stared at the new car in our driveway. The yellow Bug looked familiar, but I had no idea who'd be driving it.

Curious, I got out of the car and walked to the front door. Through the front window, I could see my mom sitting on the couch... with my guidance counselor.

As soon as I opened the door to walk inside, the room got quiet and they turned my way.

"Um... This is weird," I said.

Birdie giggled, and Mom managed a smile.

"It's nice to see you, April," Birdie said, standing up. "You have a beautiful home." She walked my way, wearing jeans with bright patches on them, red clogs, and what looked like a hand-knitted sweater, and then gave me a hug.

I awkwardly put my arms around her, sending my mom a look over her shoulder that said, *What is going on?*

Mom glanced down at her coffee and took a sip.

"Come sit with us," Birdie said, like this wasn't my house. "We were just chatting about your college applications."

My stomach sank because I knew I hadn't completed any. The last few weeks, months, years even, had been about survival. I'd avoided all the links to local colleges that Birdie sent me, trying to get by.

My mom had signed me up with a therapist at Dr. Sanders's recommendation. After two sessions, Dr. Mason already suspected I had been suffering with PTSD and anxiety since my dad's injury. It wasn't fun talking about all my feelings and traumas, but I hoped it would help get the constant feelings of guilt and pain out of my system.

But I was still depressed. Our home felt empty without Dad in it, and I felt like I didn't know how to exist without the daily occurrence of watching his moods, managing his medication, making sure Mom had enough of a break.

Even getting to do my clinical hours for my CNA certification hadn't been as fun as I thought it would be. It had me questioning everything, including my goal to become a nurse.

Mom said, "Birdie called me Friday to check in about your college applications, and when I explained some of what was going on, she was nice enough to offer to come over on her day off just to chat."

The nerves in my chest eased slightly. I could say that for Birdie; it seemed like she really did care and wasn't just cashing in a paycheck.

"I'm sorry I didn't fill out the applications," I said, looking at my mom. "I know I said I'd handle it, but I've just been overwhelmed."

"Of course you have, honey," Mom said gently.

Birdie nodded. "Senior year, college apps, ACTs and SATs. It's a hard time for any student. Especially ones carrying the types of burdens that you've been dealing with."

"My dad isn't a burden," I said quickly.

"You're right," Birdie said, sounding contrite. "I meant with the worries and concerns that you have, rightly so."

I fiddled with the seam of the velvet chair I sat on, wishing this was over. "I really will get the applications done. I can probably go to the library tomorrow and focus on them."

Mom and Birdie exchanged a glance.

"What?" I asked.

Birdie set her coffee down and leaned forward. "April, sometimes after students have had a high-pressure experience in high school, they find gap years to be quite helpful."

"Gap year? Like taking a year off?"

Birdie nodded. "Sometimes they use the year to travel to new countries or work a job and earn extra money. But mostly the time is meant to be spent discovering who you truly are and what you like."

Mom said, "You might come back and decide you still want to pursue nursing, but I was speaking with Dr. Mason the other day, and she said it's really common for people who have been trauma-tized to go into a related field that only triggers them and makes healing more difficult."

Each word they said hit me one after another, too close to home, until tears were falling down my cheeks.

"April," Mom said, getting up to comfort me, but I shook my head, letting all the stress, all the tears, out.

"I'm lost," I said finally.

Birdie nodded sympathetically. "It's normal, sweetie. I've counseled hundreds of seniors at this point. And so many of them don't know that they have options outside of going straight into college after graduation. That path works well for lots of people, but not everyone, and choosing to do something different does *not* make you a failure. Maybe you take six months and decide to enroll in December. Or you can push ahead and start in the fall. I just wanted to let you and your mom know that the option is there."

Birdie pressed herself up from the couch. "I know I just put a lot of information out there for you both, but I am here any time to help. Truly. My stepson is grown and out of the house, and I don't have any children of my own. I live to help my students."

I could feel how much she meant it.

My mom stood beside her, giving her a hug. "Thanks for everything, Birdie."

Birdie smiled, then winked at me. "Any time."

After Birdie got outside, Mom said, "That woman is something special."

And I realized I never even said thank you when she was here. "Hang on," I said, following Birdie outside.

She already had the driver's side door open on her yellow Bug.

"Birdie?" I called.

She looked up at me and waited by the door. "Did I forget something inside? I tend to do that from time to time."

I shook my head, walking closer. "I just wanted to thank you for looking out."

She nodded. "You'd be surprised how many people you have in your corner."

The way she said it made me think there was something more. "What do you mean?"

She bit her bottom lip, glancing around my driveway before facing me again. "You know that first day of school when Diego brought you to my office?"

Honestly? "I tried to forget it."

"I would too." She chuckled slightly. "But when he mentioned that thing about his sister?"

I wracked my brain and then nodded. I'd thought it was so strange, him talking about his sister when I had food all over me.

Birdie tilted her head. "Bringing you to that locker room where Sadie eats lunch? It was no coincidence."

She got into her car, and as she drove away, the words echoed in my mind.

Diego had been there for me. Even when I hated him, he'd been there for me, making my life better from the start.

## FIFTY-FIVE

## APRIL

I STAYED OUTSIDE LONGER than I needed to, just processing, before I went back inside and sat on the couch by Mom. I tucked my feet under me and leaned against her shoulder.

"What do you think about a gap year?" Mom asked, examining me. "I actually think it's a pretty good idea."

After so long living in the present, planning for the future, changing course, it didn't come naturally. "I need more time to think about it," I said.

"Of course." She nodded. "I'm sorry. I didn't mean to ambush you by that. Birdie just said she was free."

"Don't apologize." I reached up, hugging my mom, then pulled back, needing to tell her every-

364 CURVY GIRLS CAN'T DATE SURFERS

thing that had been on my heart, all the things that have felt too uncomfortable to say. "I've seen you look out for Dad and me all my life. Being a military wife is not an easy job, and these last three years especially, you've been our rock. You're the most selfless person, and I'm so lucky to be your daughter."

Mom's eyes were red and filled with tears. "April, I mean it when I say, being your mom has been the biggest privilege of my life, but I do have a regret."

Fear took hold of me, and I prayed she wouldn't regret me.

She took a breath. "I don't think I've prepared you for life after this."

"What do you mean?" I asked.

She looked out the window like she was looking at her past. "You've only known this life. The moves every few years, deployments, always meeting new, temporary people. But in less than a year, that won't be your life. You'll get to choose when you want to go... and when you want to stay."

It was a huge, expansive feeling, what Mom and Birdie had given me. The future was wide open... and it was mine to choose.

We held each other for a long time and then

decided to have a lazy afternoon, chatting and snacking and watching TV until it was time for me to pick up Heidi for our evening walk. Even though I'd been upset with Mom at first for scheduling this job for me, this was the one part of my day that had gotten me through the last few weeks.

Our house felt empty without Dad. My heart felt empty without Diego and Sadie.

But Heidi? She was there for me no matter what.

And she'd even been sticking by my side, like she knew I couldn't handle any more trouble.

But this time, when I stepped outside my house to walk to the Pfanstiels', I stopped short. Sadie was standing in the driveway, her car parked where Birdie's had been earlier. "Wh—what are you doing here?"

She kept her hands in her jacket pockets as she shrugged. "I've missed you."

Guilt swept through me. I had pulled away from Sadie, and over the last few weeks, it felt too awkward to reach back out after what a jerk I'd been. "I'm sorry. I've been a terrible friend."

Sadie smiled slightly. "Kind of."

I couldn't help but laugh. "I'm not supposed to be laughing. I should be on my knees, begging for your forgiveness, Say. I've been so awful to you." Remorse filled each of my words, and I hoped she heard how truly sorry I was.

"You were hurting. Sometimes we do things we don't mean when we're upset. Or afraid. I just hope from now on, you'll let me in instead of icing me out."

Her words carried more weight than simply being about us, but I didn't focus on the deeper meaning. "I promise I will," I said. "I missed you too."

She smiled slightly. "I'm free this evening. Do you want to hang out?"

"I'd love to." I cringed. "But I have to walk this dog..."

"I'll come with you," she said. "I can't wait to meet the infamous Heidi and see all this progress you've been making."

I laughed. The sound felt foreign to my ears but good on my heart. "Let's go."

We walked together to the Pfanstiels' house, talking about her parents' latest pottery project on the way. She invited me over to make one of my own, and I happily accepted.

"That would be great," I said, slowing at the Pfanstiels' yellow front door. "This is it." I raised my hand to knock, and as soon as the door opened, Heidi came running out, dancing around me without jumping on me.

"Hey, good girl," I said, smiling.

Jesse said, "You brought a friend. How fun."

"This is Sadie," I said.

She waved with her hand still in her jacket pocket. "Nice to meet you."

"We'll be back in an hour or so," I told him.

"Take your time. She needs to walk off the cake she just ate off our counter."

Sadie and I exchanged a look and giggled. As we walked away from the Pfanstiels', I said, "Told you she's a mess."

She reached down to scratch Heidi's ears. "I like her already,"

I held on tightly to Heidi's leash, walking from the sidewalk, over the soft sand, and then to the packed sand by the water.

"It's so pretty here," Sadie said.

I nodded, trying to remember what it felt like to see this beach for the first time. I hadn't taken time to appreciate how beautiful it was. "It's stunning," I agreed.

Sadie turned toward Diego's house, and I followed her, thinking we could turn around before we got too close. Just seeing him in the hallways at school was hard enough. Walking by his house would be... torture. Especially now that I knew how much he'd really cared about me—how much I'd messed up.

We walked in silence for a few more moments, and Sadie said, "How's your dad doing?"

My heart wrenched at the mention of my dad. I filled her in about him moving to the Rhodora Center. "We're getting good reports so far, and he seemed good when I saw him at lunch today, but it's strange, living in a home without him in it."

"That's so much," Sadie said gently. "Are you okay?"

I shrugged, not wanting to tell her how hard these last few weeks had really been. "I've missed you a lot."

Sadie nodded. "And Diego?"

"What about him?" I asked, trying not to slam up the guards around my heart.

She bit her lip. "I can tell he's miserable without you."

"He is?" My heart. My traitorous heart. This hope could break me, but I clung to it anyway.

"He doesn't smile as much. He's quieter in the classes I have with him."

Guilt made me want to disappear in the sand. "Probably because he can't play football anymore."

"I don't think that's all of it," she said.

"I was awful to him, Sadie. I pushed him away our whole relationship. I didn't even ask if he was okay after the fight."

A fresh round of guilt exploded in my stomach. I'd been right to avoid a relationship with him. Diego was everything good—sunshine and hope, all in a handsome package. I was a storm cloud to his perfect weather. We didn't belong together. No matter how much I wished we did.

There was a small smile on her face as she said, "You know you could just say you're sorry and ask him to forgive you."

I laughed. "Could it really be that easy?"

"You never know unless you try," she replied.

I lifted a corner of my mouth in a half smile, then stopped walking. We were getting too close to Diego's house. "Let's turn around."

"Okay," she said, glancing that way like she knew where he lived.

I turned and switched Heidi's leash to my other hand, but at exactly the wrong time, a seagull swooped by, and Heidi was off.

"Heidi! Come back!" I yelled, willing her to listen.

Of course, she didn't.

I sprinted after Heidi, hoping with everything I had that she would stop. Because the direction she was running?

Yeah. It was right toward Diego's house.

## FIFTY-SIX

## DIEGO

I CARRIED a surfboard to the beach for my lesson with Sadie, even though flashes of my lesson with April kept running through my mind. I tried to focus on today, because this lesson would be different with my arm still in a cast. At least I only had a couple more weeks before it came off.

Mom had helped me wrap it in plastic so no water could get in. Back when I first got injured, I told her I'd fallen down the stairs after homecoming when April broke up with me, but I doubted she believed me. She was way too good at seeing through me, but at least she didn't ask any questions.

My elbows rested on my knees, and I looked at my cast under the plastic wrap. Half our senior class had signed it. Kenzie had written her name the biggest, of course. But there was a name missing.

I wondered if I'd ever stop missing her, even if I'd accepted we wouldn't have a relationship.

If missing her would get easier when I didn't have to see her in first period every day.

Maybe the pain would be like the shoreline— always there but shifting every day. Sometimes big and wide and others covered by the waters of my life.

I looked up from my cast, trying to forget that her name wasn't there, and took a deep breath of the salty air. By the time I was surfing again, it would be winter. The water would be really cold, even with a wet suit.

But I already knew I'd get back out there. Because that's what I did.

When faced with a challenge, I rose up.

I heard panting and turned just quickly enough to see a golden ball of fur bounding up to me.

"Stop!" I said, hoping to protect my arm.

Heidi skidded to a halt, spraying sand and slobber all over me.

"Great," I said, wiping sand off my arms and trying to stay annoyed. I couldn't with her panting so happily at me. "What are you doing here?" I asked as I scratched her, and I looked up just in time to see April and Sadie jogging my way.

Seeing April in her loose sweater and leggings sent pain slicing through my chest. Strands of her dark hair had escaped from her ponytail and were wrapping around her face in the wind. Her hips swayed as she walked through the sand. And her eyes landed on me. But only for a moment.

I pushed myself up, taking hold of Heidi's leash, and walked toward the two.

Sadie mumbled something about forgetting something in her car, and I swear I saw her smile before she turned away.

Sadie didn't want to learn how to surf.

She was giving me a moment. A chance.

And I was going to make the most of it.

April reached for the leash. "Sorry, she saw a seagull."

Our hands brushed as she took the leash, sending a jolt to my heart. My body knew I couldn't let this girl go.

I wracked my mind for something, any hint of something that could convince her to give us another chance. "April..."

She looked up at me, her eyes as tumultuous as the ocean.

I steeled my chest, my heart. Because every wave had a calm spot—if you just dove deep enough.

"What are we doing?" I asked finally.

She looked from Heidi to me. "I'm sorry, I just walked too far this way. It won't happen again." She turned to walk away, but I reached for her hand.

"I meant, what are we doing staying away from each other like we don't care anymore?"

Her lips parted, but no words came out.

That was okay because I wasn't done. "I care about you, April. Even when I thought I hated you, I cared about you."

"But what does that mean?" Her voice cracked. "How could you care about me when my dad hurt you and I shoved you away? You should hate me for what I've done."

I held her hand to my chest, flattening it over my heart. "April, I stood up to your dad because I couldn't bear the thought of you being hurt. I know I probably made things worse, but you have to understand. I'd do anything for you."

Her jaw stayed strong despite the moisture

forming in her eyes. "You deserve better, Diego. So much better than what I've given you."

I held her face in my hand, wiping away a tear with my thumb. "I know it won't be easy, and there's so much for you to work through with your family... But I meant it, what I said during our lesson. I'm here for you. And even when the waves are crashing over us and it feels like they'll never stop, I..." My voice broke and I swallowed. Because even though I wanted us to get back together, I needed this to make things work. "I want you to be there for me too, even when things get hard. You can't keep running away."

Fear took hold of my body. All I'd known was moving away, saying goodbye. "I'm not even sure I know how."

"But you do," he said. "I've seen how devoted you are to your family. You'd do anything to them. And this dog." I gestured at Heidi. "She has to be the hardest dog to work with on the planet. You could have quit any time. And you stayed. You stuck it out with her, because you knew she and her family were worth it." I beat my hand on my chest. "Tell me you think I'm worth it too."

Tears poured down my cheeks as I felt every word. "Of course you're worth it." Diego had seen all my flaws, knew the ugly side of me that argued and yelled and shoved people away. He'd seen my family, been hurt by my dad. And he was only asking me one thing.

"Stay," he breathed. "Stay with me."

And then I remembered what my mom had said: I only knew the military life, but that was my parents' choice. Now the choice was mine.

And instead of fighting, instead of leaving like I'd always done... I stayed.

## FIFTY-SEVEN

## APRIL

I PUT on the dress Mom bought for me, adjusting the flowing sleeves and tying the back. Mom looked at me from the bed. "April, you look beautiful."

"Do you think Dad's going to like it?"

She nodded. "He's going to love it."

I bit my lip, looking in the mirror. "What about Diego?"

"I think he'll love the dress too," Mom said.

I shook my head, turning away from the mirror and facing her. "Do you think Dad will be okay meeting Diego?"

"His memory of him is fuzzy, and I think it will help now that Diego's out of his cast," Mom reminded me. "And I've prepped him over the last week to meet your boyfriend. Shown him pictures of

Diego and talked about how good he's been to you. Extra staff will be there too. Everything will be okay."

I wanted to believe her, but Dad's distress mattered too. I wanted him to feel comfortable in his new home, not like we were ambushing him.

The doorbell rang, and I jumped.

It had been so long since we could use the doorbell. But my boyfriend was at the door. And he was ringing the bell. Things changed all the time.

I took a deep breath and focused on the items in the room, reminding me where I was like my therapist had taught me to do. She called it grounding myself in the present, which really helped with my PTSD symptoms.

Mom said, "I need to touch up my makeup. I'll meet you two in the car?"

I nodded. "See you in a bit."

I held on to the banister as I walked down the stairs and went to the front door. Diego looked great in dark jeans and a Henley, holding an arrangement of fruit covered in chocolate.

"Diego, that's so sweet. You didn't have to do that."

"You said this is his favorite, and I couldn't exactly bring him flowers."

I reached up on my toes and kissed his cheek. "Thank you," I whispered. "But who says guys don't like flowers?"

He thought it over for a moment. "You know? That would be nice. Why haven't you bought me flowers yet?"

Laughing, I grabbed my purse and Mom's keys off the hook by the door and started walking to the door. "We have plenty of time for that."

Even though it was winter in Emerson, the air felt like spring used to in Kansas. Crisp. Especially with the moisture from the ocean permeating the air.

"Anything I need to know?" Diego asked as we stood by the car.

"We've prepped Dad for your visit, and he seems okay, but his body might remember your last interaction. If things start to escalate, I need you to leave the room."

I could see the pain in his eyes as he opened his mouth to protest.

"There will be staff there," I continued, "to step in so you don't have to." I reached up and smoothed the collar of his shirt. "The doctor thinks with regular visits, my dad will get to know you. I want him to know you as the wonderful guy you are."

He nodded, his jaw clenching. "I hope he doesn't hate me. After everything."

We both knew what 'everything' was. It was in our past. "Enjoy the magic of the moment, remember?"

His eyes warmed, and he bent to kiss my forehead. "Thank you."

The front door opened, and my mom walked down the front steps toward us. "Have I mentioned how cute you two are together?"

I smiled at her. "Only a million times."

"Half a million," she replied, going to the front door of the car.

I sat up front with her, and Diego rode in the back seat. Mom tried to make small talk about the last football game of the season coming up next week, but we were all tense. Nervous.

A nurse met us at the center and walked with us to Dad's room, letting us know they'd reminded him about our visit this morning.

I linked hands with Diego, squeezing tightly. His grip was solid, comforting.

We could do this.

*We could do this.*

The nurse slowed in front of Dad's open door, now with the permanent golden name plate, and knocked softly. "Doug, you have visitors."

"Come in," he called.

Mom went through the door first. "Hi, honey. April brought her boyfriend to meet you. Last time was a little rough, but I'm hoping you two can get along."

I heard Dad say, "Why was it rough?"

He didn't remember the fight, probably because of the sedative. It hurt, knowing his injury had taken such a toll. But I hoped he and Diego would make the most of their second chance at a first impression.

Mom said, "You got a little angry—you know how you do sometimes—and he stepped in to keep April safe."

"I would never hurt Ape."

"I know," she replied.

I looked up at Diego, his eyes misting over.

"But that's good, he looks out for her," Dad said. Now my eyes were glistening too.

I squeezed Diego's hand.

"Are they here?" Dad asked.

I pulled Diego through the door. "Hey, Dad. This is us."

# EPILOGUE

SADIE

I USED to hate the idea of a football game. With social anxiety, being packed into the bleachers with everyone from school plus their families was pretty much torture.

But it was easier to handle when I went with April. I didn't have to worry about who to talk to or if I'd embarrass myself, because she already knew me. And she didn't judge me for being a little awkward or different. It turned out football games could even be fun, cheering for the team and having concession food, which was definitely an underrated high school delicacy.

This was the last football game of the season, the last one I'd ever be able to attend as an Emerson Academy student. And even though high school always felt like it was dragging by at a snail's pace, I couldn't believe we were here... already at the end of football season. Almost halfway through the year.

Mr. Davis's voice came through the loudspeakers. "Now we have a special guest to perform the national anthem as a gift from Diego De Leon to April Adams."

April's eyes widened as she looked from the field where Diego was smiling at her to the announcers' booth. Through the window, I could barely see...

"Without further ado, Jude Santiago and Desirae De Leon!"

I had to cover my ears; April screamed so loud. She bounced on her toes, tears streaming down her cheeks as they sang the national anthem. And when Des and Jude walked our way, I kept my hands ready to catch April in case she fainted.

Des remembered me from school, which was a surprise, and she and Jude were so sweet to April. They sat with us for a few minutes until they joined the rest of the De Leons in the front row of the stands.

I could see April's eyes flicking from them to the field throughout the game.

The horn went off, meaning someone made a

touchdown, and April and I stood up with the rest of the crowd, clapping our hands together.

Everyone stayed on their feet, counting down the last ten seconds of the game.

TEN

NINE

EIGHT

SEVEN

SIX

FIVE

"I can't believe this is it," April said beside me.

"I know."

TWO

ONE

Someone shot off a confetti cannon, sending pieces of paper raining over the stands. I smiled in wonder, catching the colorful pieces as they fell down. It was like magic.

"Let's go talk to Diego," April said.

I nodded, walking beside her with the rest of the crowd swarming the field. We quickly found Diego, wearing jeans and his jersey. That cast had come off last weekend, but he still wasn't cleared to play.

He opened his arms when he saw April and me

and took her in a hug, resting his cheek against the top of her head.

Then she hit his arm. "YOU GOT JUDE SANTIAGO TO SING AT MY HIGH SCHOOL AND YOU DIDN'T TELL ME? I'M NOT EVEN WEARING EYELINER!"

There was so much mirth in his eyes as he laughed at April. "You wouldn't wear eyeliner for me?"

"That's not the point," she muttered.

"Don't worry," he said, "they're at my house all weekend before they leave for on tour. You'll get to hang out with him with your eyeliner on."

"I think I'm going to faint," April said to no one in particular.

I only laughed. I liked Jude's music, but I wasn't the kind to fangirl over mainstream musicians.

Diego winked at me. "I played a great game, right, Sadie?"

I laughed. Leave it to Diego to make a joke about not being able to play. He could find gold in any amount of dirt. April smirked up at him.

"I didn't mind watching you from behind," she said.

My cheeks instantly flamed. I was so not good at

flirting, and hearing her do it so easily just reminded me how out of place I was on the high school dating scene. Not that there were any guys in my school lining up for the opportunity to date me. Not even close.

Terrell came by, giving Diego a high five with his free hand. His jersey was off, showing just his tight undershirt clinging to his solid torso.

"You played great," Diego said, a hint of emotion in his voice despite the joking earlier.

"Thanks, man," Terrell said. Then he smiled at April and me. "Last football game of high school. Can you believe it?"

April shook her head. "Not one bit."

I nodded. "Are you looking forward to basketball?" Even though I didn't go to the games, my head wasn't so far under a rock that I didn't know about Terrell's skills on the court. He was good at football, but he was *great* at basketball. People who knew more about the sport than me expected him to go pro after college.

Terrell's grin showed straight white teeth and contagious excitement. "I can't freaking wait."

April said, "Sadie and I will have to come and watch you play! I've actually been having fun going to the games."

"Actually," Diego muttered at the same time Terrell met my eyes.

"That would be great," he said.

I swore he was talking just to me. Why?

"You guys wanna go to Waldo's?" Terrell asked.

April and I exchanged a look, deciding silently. I liked how she checked in on me. After a few months as friends, she knew my social battery could deplete pretty quickly. Finally, I nodded.

Terrell grinned. "Awesome. I'm gonna shower. See you all there?"

We nodded, and then Diego gave April a quick kiss goodbye, saying he was going to get his things from the locker room.

April and I started walking toward her car, and she bumped my arm. "Am I missing something? If I didn't know any better, I'd say Terrell was flirting with you!"

I made a laugh between a cackle and a snort. (You can imagine how attractive that was.)

"Why are you laughing?"

"Because that's ridiculous. Imagine it. *High school basketball star dates girl who hides in the locker room during lunch.*"

"I mean, a high school football star dated me," she said, a dopey smile on her face. "And he got his super famous sister and future brother-in-law to sing the national anthem for me."

"Yes, and I'm happy for you. Let's just enjoy your happily ever after without worrying about mine." Because if I knew one thing, it was that I was not the kind of girl who fell in love. Not in high school anyway and certainly not with a guy like Terrell.

Want to see where Diego and April are one year later? Grab the free bonus story today!

Visit my website to get alerts about Sadie and Terrell's story.

GET THE BONUS STORY

GET UPDATES ON KELSIE'S NEXT BOOK

## AUTHOR'S NOTE

The more I've learned about trauma and childhood wounds, the more I want to advocate for both healing and understanding. And the longer you live life, the greater the chance that you'll face unspeakable demons.

April's wounds... they were severe. And many of them are similar to my own. Watching someone you love experience trauma like what her father did, sometimes that can scar like you experienced it yourself.

You feel... helpless. Scared. Guilty. Angry.

So many things that are hard to piece together.

And all those feelings? They shape the way you view the world.

The worst part is that when something terrible

happens, you can't contribute your fears to mere anxiety, because you know that horrible things can and do happen, even to people like you.

For April, watching her dad reduced by an injury he couldn't control and she couldn't help? That was absolutely world shaking. It made her withdraw from other people because she was afraid of being abandoned, worried about being unable to help. It made her slip into self-preservation mode, which often led to even more painful decisions. Ones that hurt her and those around her.

What she couldn't see in the moment through her trauma was how much she was missing out on by closing herself off to relationships, both platonic and romantic. Because really good relationships? They can be so healing.

They can help you trust.

Help you have fun, which is a key to feeling safe again.

Help you believe that even though bad things are possible, good things are possible too.

And that hope? It's everything.

It helps you put one foot in front of the other, even when all you feel like is giving up.

If you're having a hard time right now, I hope you'll keep an open heart and open mind to the good that can come into your life. The light that can shine through all the broken cracks of your heart. It won't be easy—it'll probably be scary as hell, but you can be tough as nails while feeling tender as paper thin glass.

Flowers still grow through sidewalk cracks.

## ACKNOWLEDGMENTS

Writing in the Curvy Girl Club always feels like hanging out with old friends, and I'm so happy I have so many people helping me out along the way!

My wonderful husband, who may not be a surfer boy but who has ridden many waves with me. His continual support of my writing is part of the reason I'm typing this today.

My boys are endlessly supportive and always give me the best title ideas. (Curvy Girls Can't Date T-Rexes is among my top five!)

Team Kelsie! As my readership has grown, so has my team. Annie and Sally are so incredibly talented and fun to work with. They are amazing partners on this incredible journey, and I can't wait to see the heights we can reach as a team.

I'm convinced my editor, Tricia Harden, is one of the best humans out there. She's kind, thoughtful, and so supportive of my writing. I'm so lucky to have her in my corner.

Najla Qamber nailed it once again with this cover! I can't wait to show you all the incredible work she has coming for me!

Major thanks to Courtney Encheff and Filipe Valente who are bringing this audiobook to life! Hearing the story aloud is always so much fun!

Although I always wanted to take a CNA class, I never got around to it. Luckily, my brother, Dakota Hoss had the experience and expertise to help me out! The cute eating scene would not be there without his idea! I also got tons of help from the 4YourCNA channel on YouTube!

Thanks to Lance Maxwell who gave my son and me our first ever surf lesson! It was so useful in writing my favorite scene of this book!

My sweet readers in Kelsie Stelting: Readers Club are the absolute best. We lift each other up, share fun stories, and hang out online. They make being a writer so much fun.

And to you, the person reading this note. I love your interest in the story and my words here. As someone who often felt like her voice wasn't heard, this has been so healing, and your time reading means the absolute world to me.

# GLOSSARY

*LATIN PHRASES*

**Ad Meliora:** School motto meaning "toward better things."

**Audentes fortuna iuvat:** Motto of *Dulce Periculum* meaning "Fortune favors the bold."

**Dulce Periculum:** means "danger is sweet" - local secret club that performs stunts

**Multum in Parvo:** means "much in little"

*LOCATIONS*

**Town Name:** Emerson

**Location:** Halfway between Los Angeles and San Francisco

**Surrounding towns:** Brentwood, Seaton, Heywood

**Emerson Academy:** Private school Rory and Beckett attend

**Brentwood Academy:** Rival private school

**Walden Island:** Tourism island off the coast, only accessible by helicopter or ferry

**Laughlin:** Small country between England and Scotland formed in the early 1900s.

**MacColl:** Capital city of Laughlin where the royal family resides.

*MAIN HANGOUTS*

**Emerson Elementary Library:** Where Rory tutors Anna, open to students K-7

**Emerson Field:** Massive park in the center of Emerson

**Emerson Memorial:** Local hospital

**Emerson Shoppes:** Shopping mall

**Emerson Trails:** Hiking trails in Emerson, near Emerson Field

**Halfway Café:** Expensive dining option in Emerson, frequented by celebrities

**La La Pictures:** Movie theater in Emerson

**Ripe:** Major health food store serving the tri-city area

**Roasted:** Popular coffee shop in Emerson

JJ Cleaning: Cleaning service owned by Jordan's mom

**Seaton Bakery:** Delicious dining and drink option in Seaton where Beckett works

**Seaton Beach:** Beach near Seaton – rougher than the beach near Brentwood

**Seaton Pier:** Fishing pier near Seaton

**Spike's:** Local 18-and-under club

**Waldo's Diner:** local diner, especially popular after sporting events

*APPS*

**Rush+:** Game app designed by Kai Rush and his father

**Sermo**: chat app used by private school students

*IMPORTANT ENTITIES*

**Bhatta Productions:** Production company owned by Zara's father

**Brentwood Badgers:** Professional football team

**Heywood Market:** Big ranch/distributor where everyone can purchase their meat locally

**Invisible Mountains:** Local major nonprofit - Callie's dad is the CEO

**Dugan Industries:** Owns and manages Brentwood Marina, along with other entities. Owned by Ryker Dugan's father, Trent Dugan.

## The Curvy Girl Club

Curvy Girls Can't Date Quarterbacks

Curvy Girls Can't Date Billionaires

Curvy Girls Can't Date Cowboys

Curvy Girls Can't Date Bad Boys

Curvy Girls Can't Date Best Friends

Curvy Girls Can't Date Bullies

Curvy Girls Can't Dance

Curvy Girls Can't Date Soldiers

Curvy Girls Can't Date Princes

Curvy Girls Can't Date Rock Stars

Curvy Girls Can't Date Surfers

Curvy Girls Can't Date Curvy Girls (Pride Edition)

## The Texas High Series

Chasing Skye

Becoming Skye

Loving Skye

Always Anika

## New at Texas High

Abi and the Boy Next Door

Abi and the Boy Who Lied

Abi and the Boy She Loves

## The Pen Pal Romance Series

Dear Adam

Fabio Vs. the Friend Zone

Sincerely Cinderella

## Standalone Novels

Road Trip with the Enemy: A Sweet Standalone
Romance

## YA Contemporary Romance Anthologies

The Art of Taking Chances

Two More Days

## Nonfiction

Raising the West

## ABOUT THE AUTHOR

Kelsie Stelting is a body positive romance author who writes love stories with strong characters, deep feelings, and happy endings.

She currently lives in Colorado with her family. You can often find her writing, spending time with family, and soaking up too much sun wherever she can find it.

**Visit www.kelsiestelting.com to get a free story and sign up for her readers' group!**

facebook.com/kelsiesteltingcreative

twitter.com/kelsiestelting

instagram.com/kelsiestelting

Made in United States
Troutdale, OR
10/24/2023

13949032R00230